D1067067

Debit et Gravé par G. Bruiffordus 54.

LOST REALMS

Text by
Robert Holdstock & Malcolm Edwards

Illustrated by
John Avon, Bill Donohoe,
Godfrey Dowson, Dick French, Mark Harrison,
Michael Johnson, Pauline Martin,
David O'Connor, Colleen Payne,
Scitex 350, Carolyn Scrace.

Paper Tiger

A Dragon's World Ltd Imprint

Dragon's World Ltd
High Street
Limpsfield
SURREY RH8 0DY
Great Britain

First published 1984
Reprinted 1991

Copyright Dragon's World Ltd 1984
Copyright text Robert Holdstock and
Malcolm Edwards 1984
Copyright illustrations Dragon's World Ltd 1984

*No part of this book may be reproduced in any form or by any
electronic or mechanical means, including information storage and
retrieval systems, without permission in writing from Dragon's World
Ltd, except by a reviewer who may quote brief passages in a review.*

All rights reserved.

Caution. All images are copyrighted by Dragon's World Ltd or
by publishers acknowledged in the text. Their use in any form
without prior written permission from Dragon's World Ltd or
the appropriate copyright holder is strictly forbidden.

Limpback: ISBN 0 905895 91 6

Printed in Singapore

Contents

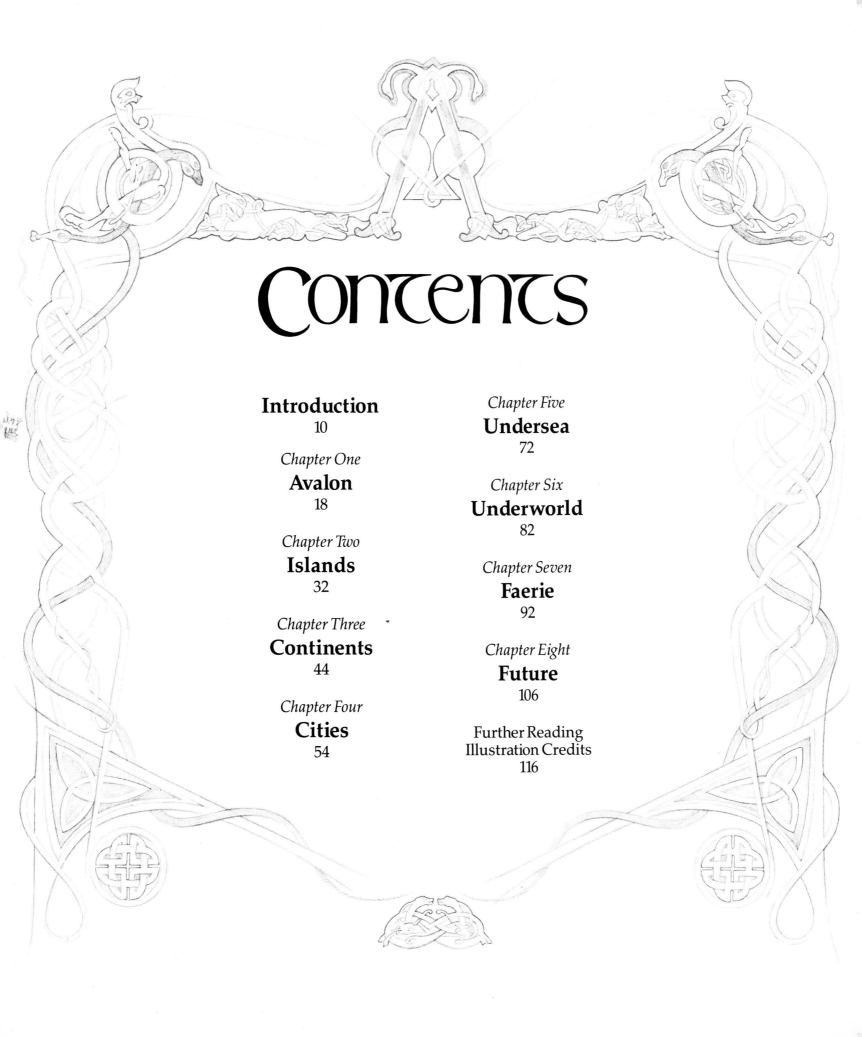

INTRODUCTION

It is easy today to think that we know all there is to know about our world. Explorers have visited almost every corner of the planet. Areas which only a hundred years ago were mysterious blanks on the maps are now tamed and exploited for their resources. High resolution photographs taken from orbiting satellites can show almost every square yard of the land's surface in fine detail.

Yet it remains true to say that what is hidden remains a mystery. If there are places which cannot be found on ordinary maps, then they cannot be revealed by ordinary photographs. If there were once lands – now vanished – which have become fable rather than part of accepted history, they may be no less real simply because we do not generally accept their existence.

This is a book about such places: about vanished realms of antiquity; about realms which may still exist, hidden from our inquisitive eyes; about realms which may never have existed – though who can say for certain? – about realms lost to us because they have not yet come to be.

The archaeological and historical record of our past will never be complete. Too much has been lost; too much has been destroyed. In our cities we know there is a wealth of information hidden just under the surface, but we cannot get at it – except briefly and in fragments – without demolishing the places where we live. In some areas we can still see the evidence of past habitation, but in others there is nothing to indicate the vanished past until some accident suddenly reveals it.

In some instances we know how very fragmentary our knowledge is. We know of the huge lost libraries in, for example, Constantinople – where in the fourteenth century a hundred thousand books were burnt by the invading Turks, the great majority of them probably never to be seen again. We know how little survives from the work of the great writers of classical Greece and Rome. We are rightly grateful to have some examples of writings from the remote past – such as the *Epic of Gilgamesh*, the earliest known work of literature, from the third millennium BC. Yet who knows what great literary tradition might have flourished of which *Gilgamesh* was but a part; and who knows what other great civilizations there might have been in antiquity which are now lost to us much more completely than the one which produced this great epic?

If no artifacts survive, though, some other element often does. It is the element which becomes absorbed into fable and legend, into folktale and epic. Myths and legends may seem to be no more than collections of colourful and fanciful stories, in which people ignorant of the world seek to account for its mysteries by

inventing pantheons of gods and strange creatures, performing mighty deeds. But there is much more to it than that. As students of myth know, such stories can, when analysed, tell us a lot about the society that created them – about its laws and taboos, its people and their hopes and fears, its achievements and defeats. In a society whose tales are passed on through the oral tradition these tales generally become distorted or transmuted, but the kernel of truth remains. Among those stories must lie accounts of realms now lost to us, and some of those that we think mere fanciful invention may in truth be places which did exist, somewhere, at some time.

Examples abound. Many are dealt with in the body of this book, but a few others can be mentioned here. There is, for example, one of the oldest realms, and one which by its nature is more permanently lost to us than any other: Eden, the earthly paradise, the realm of primeval innocence.

Can any myth match Eden for its ability to fascinate and intrigue the human imagination? A legendary garden in which the first man and woman are placed, to lead an idyllic life – no death, no need to hunt, no need for modesty – as long as they do not *question* the higher province of God. The fall from grace – the discovery of original sin – symbolizes so much. On the one hand, the story says that the first humans, by falling prey to temptation and wickedness, lost out on paradise; on the other hand, from our perspective, we may say that plucking the apple from the Tree of Knowledge was the first example of that curiosity which makes us greater than animals. It was the beginning of the human race.

Was Eden a mere memory of the lush savannahs on which the last of the "apemen" became the first humans? Could it have been something much more outlandish: a memory of the study cage of an alien race who implanted the seed of higher awareness in a selected few human animals? This was an idea effectively dramatized in the film *2001: A Space Odyssey*, and one which is not to be dismissed out of hand, however far-fetched it might seem: other, more "natural" accounts of the acquisition of true intelligence require equal suspension of disbelief. The story of Eden is so simple that it can be interpreted in a thousand ways, from historical to religious, from serious to whimsical. It is an example of how an ancient, almost archetypal memory – of a "beginning place", or a time when humankind was closer to nature – becomes adapted to reflect the more precise concepts of different cultures. Eden is very much a Hebew and Sumerian idyll, but to the ancient Greeks it was the "Hesperides", the Garden of the Daughters of the Evening, believed to have been located in the isolated valley of Arcady. To the Greeks, too, there were the Elysian Fields, in the Underworld. To the Celts there were Avalon and Lyonesse – both reflections of the racial longing for an ideal place, a place from antiquity where an early – or first – human form emerged.

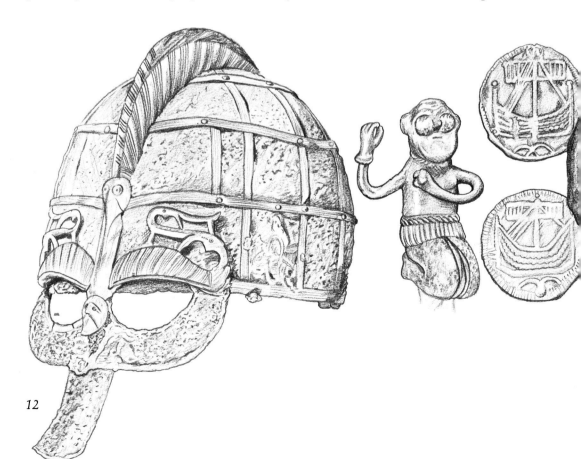

Eden has been located all over the world by different writers, and even, in some cases, on other worlds, notably Venus. But if there was a real Eden – an actual place from which the stories sprang – it seems most probable that it was located in the alluvial plain between the rivers Tigris and Euphrates, the site of the ancient civilization of Sumeria. Here was a lush and fertile area in the midst of what was otherwise barren and inhospitable desert. Here, too, was one of the oldest of human societies. But locating the physical area is only part of the quest. Eden is an idea as much as it is a place, and it is an idea which lives on. Many of the lost realms described in this book have elements of Eden in them. They are places free from the dirt, disease and unrest of our world. They are lands whose inhabitants have regained – or have never lost – the serenity and innocence that was to have been the birthright of all humans until we were expelled from Eden.

Other realms are not quite so widely known, but are still persuasive examples of the places which we know only as a mix of fiction, history, legend and imagination. We can see how fragments of travellers' tales, coupled with an immense hunger to know about the blank spots on the map, gave rise to tales of realms which – if they did truly exist – exist now only as legend. One such is the realm of Prester John.

Prester John is today a largely forgotten name, yet for more than four hundred years – from the middle of the twelfth century to the end of the sixteenth – the existence of his Empire was an article of faith throughout Western Europe, and countless travellers, adventurers and ambassadors set out in search of it.

The story reached Europe first in 1145, when the Pope learned from one of his bishops of the existence of a priest-king, John, ruling over a vast empire somewhere in India (a name which then took in most of Asia and Africa). John was a Christian (thanks to the efforts of the apostle Thomas), and he was willing to raise an army to aid in the Crusades.

Confirmation arrived in the form of a letter from the mighty Prester John himself, sent simultaneously to the Emperors of Rome and Byzantium. It revealed that he was ruler of an immense country, rich in gold and precious stones. Forty-two Christian kings were under his sway.

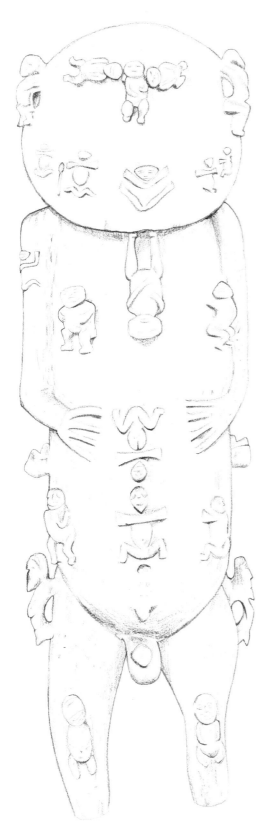

His was an exotic and wonderful country. There were to be found gryphons and unicorns, and wild hares as big as sheep. There were men with horns and three or four eyes at the back of their heads. There were magic herbs and stones, and anthropophagi and centaurs. There were ten of the lost tribes of Israel.

None of this seemed particularly unreasonable in the twelfth and thirteenth centuries, and a succession of travellers – among them Marco Polo – set out to journey to his kingdom, wherever it might be. They found strange and wonderful civilizations in China and the East, but they did not find Prester John. The location of his kingdom changed as map-makers learned more about the world beyond the Mediterranean, but there were still plenty of unaccounted-for areas in which to place it. For a time it was in Tibet; later it was shifted for a considerable period to Ethiopia; much later still it was gradually forgotten.

Yet the story cannot have been conjured out of thin air, though it may have been exaggerated in many of its particulars as it was passed from teller to teller. It is now thought that Prester John's letter was a forgery, but that cannot be proved. Perhaps somewhere in Asia in the twelfth century there *was* a mighty Christian king; perhaps he *did* command a court of 30,000 nobles; perhaps they *did* dine, once a day, at a table built of solid emerald, supported on columns of amethyst.

There are other examples of equally enduring tales which describe countries for which there is no historical evidence, yet which cannot be dismissed as mere fabrication. There is, for example, the country of the Amazons, accepted as fact by historians of the classical Greek period such as Herodotus and Plato. The Amazons were a nation ruled over by a Queen, whose parliament and soldiery were all female. They were supposed to live somewhere on the shores of the Black Sea, but when this proved not to be the case their location was shifted into the Caucasus Mountains. Again, they were not found when the Persians under Alexander the Great conquered the region, and later accounts put them as far away as Central Asia.

Wherever the land of the Amazons was, it certainly does seem to have existed. Many Greek historians give sober accounts of the invasion of Greece by the Amazons, who were only defeated by King Theseus after they had reached and occupied Athens itself. It is hard to imagine that this is just a folktale.

Perhaps the most pervasive of all lost worlds stories in relatively recent history is that of Atlantis, an island, or a country, or a continent, which sank below the sea in a great cataclysm – which may have been the Biblical deluge – destroying its civilization. It was first referred to in known literature by Plato, and has been hunted without provable success for more than two thousand years. On the way it has become perhaps the most symbolic of all lost realms.

Just as Eden cannot be found – because it can only be found by losing ourselves, abandoning what makes us truly human – so Atlantis cannot properly be found, for Atlantis today is more than just a mysterious vanished civilization. It represents things important to the human psyche: the elements of lost ancient wisdom, and things which are just beyond our grasp. We need to know that there are still discoveries to be made; curiosity about the unknown is essential to us. Nothing could bring about the downfall of the human race much more certainly than the knowledge that there was nothing left for us to find out.

Tales of lost realms like Atlantis – and like the realms we visit in this book – may become embroidered as time goes on to maintain their strangeness. They must always contain some element more strange than what we already know – otherwise what is the point of searching for them. To a great extent it is the search itself which is the source of excitement: the finding and sifting of evidence, the hunting for clues. If some or all of these places exist, it is best, perhaps, that we do not find them. An El Dorado is more exciting to the human imagination than a Machu Picchu. The latter, dramatic and interesting as it is, is known; its secrets are revealed; it is another stop on the tourist itinerary. Until it is discovered, though, there is more than one El Dorado: there are as many as there are human imaginations to dream of its wonders.

This book is a collection of those dreams.

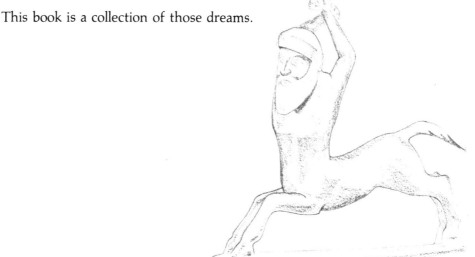

Avalon

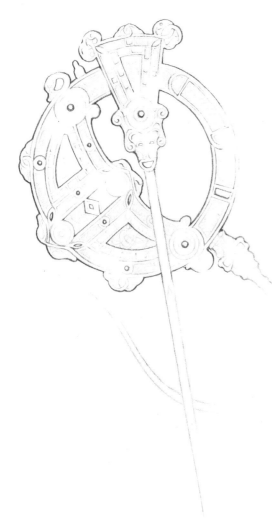

In about the year 540 AD a violent battle was fought on the banks of a river, at a place called Camlann, which was perhaps in Cornwall. The battle may have been fought over a territorial dispute, or over tribute unpaid, or because of treachery; perhaps the violent interface between two religions was the issue. In any event, both warleaders fell, each fatally wounded. Legend holds that one was called Medraut. The other was a man who had been well versed in the techniques of Roman war; he had adapted the Roman style of cavalry to a tight-knit unit of men and for thirty years had held the west-country borders of Britain against the expansionist tendencies of the Saxon overlords of the east. According to a writer called Nennius, in battle he carried the image of the Virgin Mary upon his shield. Legend tells us that this man's name was Arthur.

Arthur, Dragonlord of the Britons. A Romanised Celt, brought up under the dual influence of the new Christianity and the old religion of earth, moon and nature gods. On that cold dawn in 540 he received a fatal wound from his kinsman, Medraut, and was taken away to die with dignity.

This is how a later story tells of it:
"Then Sir Bedevere took the king upon his back, and so went with him to that water side. And when they were at the water side, fast by the bank hoved a little barge with many fair ladies in it, and among them was a queen, and they all had black hoods, and all wept and shrieked when they saw King Arthur.
"Now put me in the barge," said the King.
"And so he did, softly; and there received him three queens with great mourning.
"Then Sir Bedevere cried, 'Ah my Lord Arthur, what shall become of me, now ye go from me and leave me here alone among mine enemies?'
"'Comfort thyself,' said the King. 'And do as well as thou mayest, for in me is no trust for to trust in; for I will into the vale of Avilion to heal me of my grievous wound: and if thou hear never more of me, pray for my soul.'"

Thomas Malory wrote his epic cycle *Le Morte D'Arthur* from prison, in the fourteenth century. It is a fabulous combination of flimsy fact, broad belief, and imaginative excursion. Tennyson advanced upon Malory; the Pre-Raphaelites, Rosetti and Burne-Jones in particular, visually interpreted the tales of the Knights of the Round Table, and all of these between them have created the image of a King, clad in bright armour, his Knights neither pure (save the saintly Sir Galahad) nor evil, but all desperate to find the chalice of the Last Supper: the Holy Grail.

The images and the characters in this fiction resonate mythically: Lancelot, Bedevere, Galahad, the beautiful Guinevere, the Castle at Camelot, Merlin the Magician, Uther Pendragon, and Morgan le Fay, the dark side of faerie. And of course, there is the end of things, the final scene: Arthur returning to the lake from which a naiad – the Lady of the Lake – had given him his sword Caliburn (or Excalibur, depending upon your source) there to be transported by a barge rowed by three black-robed women, to the far shore of the place. Here, his wounds would heal; here he would wait until called upon to return to England; in this hidden realm he would rest in a cave until called upon to lead his country in triumphant battle; the place of the dead. A mystic valley. Avalon!

It is impossible to think of Avalon without Arthur; few people can think of Arthur without considering Avalon. The nature of Arthur's death, that is, his transportation to a realm where there *is* no death, is one of the most potent images of the vulgate mediaeval folk cycle, an incident – briefly enough described in itself – that resonates with all religion and mysticism. He is the King who will return, the warlord who is the Once and Future King, to be reincarnated at a future time. The survival of the spirit, the return to life of the Great in Deed, is far more a Celtic philosophy than a Christian one, and is a dim echo of an early belief associated with the Indo-European culture that not only gave rise to most European languages as we know them, but spread east. There, that belief was developed into the Hindu concept of reincarnation. Indeed, the Celtic *druid* – man of wisdom – and the Indian Brahmin are of the same genesis.

The legend of Arthur and his Knights, of Guinevere and the Grail, and of his death in mysterious Avalon, is not a single folk tale "writ large". It is a brilliant fusion of history, ancient myth and folk-lore, mediaeval whim, and Christian "cleansing" of pre-Christian beliefs. The tale that Malory told, the classic story of the Knights of the Round Table, is a fusion of scores of individual myths, a hundred fire-side fictions fitted together with skill, and at a time several centuries removed from the historical genesis of those particular fictions.

Guinevere the Queen, for example, was merely an earth goddess of the Celts – Gwenhwyfar. Lancelot is Breton fabrication. Percival, Kay, Galahad, all of these are reflections of the same warrior principle which later became associated with Arthur. In earlier Celtic stories they are known as Peredur, Pryderi, Pwyll, Goronwy, even "Arthur". The Grail? A fantasy to do with the vial in which Christ's blood was collected by Joseph of Arimethea (later developed into the Chalice used at the Last Supper, but derived from the legend of the Cauldron of Plenty, into which a dead warrior was placed to restore his life).

When all is said and done, only two historical – which is to say *real* – elements of the fable remain. One is Arthur himself. The other is the Isle of Avalon, to which he was taken for burial.

To understand Arthur, and to begin to discover where the lost realm of Avalon lies, it is necessary to review the historical events in Britain from the year 700 BC. This was the approximate time that the first Celtic clans were settling in these islands, migrating from their homelands in Switzerland. They brought iron weapons, which were far superior to the bronze of the tribes they conquered.

They traded extensively in Europe, and developed a fine, artistic culture. Their wars were local, tribal affairs; they hunted boar, bear and enemy heads. They enjoyed feasting, worshipped nature gods, especially the antlered Lord of Animals, a Moon Goddess strongly associated with horses, and a mystic Earth Goddess. They told tall tales of heroic warriors and chiefs: Peredur, Bran, Cu chullain.

The Romans invaded Britain in 41 AD and soon were co-existing peacefully. But in 410 AD the legions withdrew to Rome, leaving Britain vulnerable to the Irish, the Scots and particularly the Germanic peoples: the Jutes, the Angles and the Saxons. By the year 450 a ferocious war of conquest and defence was under way in what we now think of as England. Anglo-Saxons fought westwards against a retreating defensive line of Romanised Celts.

The literature of the time, and later, celebrates a Warchief called Ambrosius Aurelianus, who was very effective at keeping the Saxons at bay. But it was a second Warchief who was responsible for establishing the final defensive line, from Somerset, north along the Welsh borders, and up to Hadrian's Wall. Several fierce battles were fought in the early 500s AD and were won by the Britons. The Saxons were turned back, and began to settle the English lowlands. The border against the Germanic peoples held for thirty years or so, despite skirmishes.

Who was this Chieftain? Who was the man who capitalised on Aurelianus's beginnings, united the Celtic tribes and could hold a border of more than 600 miles? The Welsh monk Nennius is in no doubt when he writes his disparaging tome *History of the Britons*:

"Then Arthur fought against those men in those days with the kings of the Britons, but he was the leader of battles...
The eighth battle was at the fort of Guinnon, in which Arthur carried the image of the blessed Mary, ever-virgin, on his shoulders and the pagans were put to flight...
The twelfth battle was at Badon Hill where nine hundred and sixty men perished at one charge of Arthur's and no-one killed them save he himself..."

The *Mabinogion*, a collection of early Welsh tales, tells much of Arthur's exploits, hunting giant boars and suchlike. Arthur as a name became immensely popular in the late 500s AD. But this is only circumstantial evidence for the existence of an historical Arthur, and there are pointers against that existence; for example the Christian monk Gildas, writing well after Arthur's death, refers only to Ambrosius Aurelianus, a strange, indeed suspicious omission if Arthur had been a real hero.

Perhaps Aurelianus had a nickname: Artus, The Bear. Arthur, in parallel with Peredur, Bran, Owein and the rest, may have been a legendary Celtic figure, much spoken of in tales, whose *attributes* were attached to stories of Aurelianus to form the first legends.

In a way it is unimportant whether this unknown Chieftain was called Arthur, or so-named after the events during a "fusion" with earlier legends. The fact of his existence is demonstrable simply by looking at the wars of the time, and the establishment of a thirty year peace. He was a charismatic man who developed – or should that be *re*-developed – two things to enable him to win time from the Saxon fire-storm: a cavalry unit, and an appeal to the minds of the Celtic tribes.

The Roman cavalry was one of the most formidable in Europe, chiefly because of its discipline. The Roman presence in Britain brought an appreciation of the horse as something a lot more important than an animal to pull chariots. What they didn't bring was the stirrup. That particular invention didn't get to Britain until the seventh century. Or did it? What, after all, is a stirrup except a leg support to help with balance in the saddle? It is a pair of loops, for the toe, or the foot, or the knee, and some simple sling support would have been ideal for sleeping in that saddle on long rides.

Did the Britons turn from breeding hunting dogs to breeding horses? With fresh horses and staging posts along the border, and with a rudimentary stirrup for speed and support, a small cavalry unit could have patrolled the whole border in twenty days. The most important thing here is that the Chieftain, the Warlord, could be *seen*, and could inspire and encourage his clans across a greater distance. Carrying the image of the Virgin Mary, did Arthur bring a Christian resolve to the essentially Celtic tribes, holding them to the faith, determinedly opposing the pagan Saxons? This question will be returned to later.

The stories of Arthur are celebrated in several sources, and were certainly part of British folk-lore by the eighth century AD. It is in the hands of the Christian writers, however, that the chivalrous romance begins to develop – the anonymous *Death of Arthur*, written about 1245 AD; Chretian de Troye's several works, including *Lancelot*; Geoffrey of Monmouth's ostensibly "historical" book *The History of the Kings of Britain*; all of which were part of the basis for Malory's *Le Morte D'Arthur*. Whatever the sources – now lost – that began this epic cycle, the Celtic influence is unmistakable. Almost every detail of Arthurian romance can be traced back to the Celtic vision of gods, warriors, magic and the Otherworld. Earth goddesses become queens. Morgan Le Fay, for example, is the early Celtic Morrigan, a raven-haired triple goddess, with a strongly sexual role in mythology, but who was more concerned with divination of the outcome of wars, and with shape-shifting into a raven in order to patrol the field of battle. Morgan loses none of this implied black magic in the Arthurian epics.

The Holy Grail can be linked with sacrificial cups, or cauldrons. The Knights reflect the concept of cavalry, their individual quests being typical of Celtic folklore, where warriors adventure abroad against the supernatural. Gawain and the Green Knight alludes directly to the Celtic worship of the Head, which was imbued with great powers, and able to communicate after being severed. Percival seems linked with a strongly established Welsh legendary figure, Peredur or Pryderi, who was once clearly a hero figure of immense popularity; Pryderi's exploits parallel Arthur's in many ways, testifying to the later fusion of history and myth. The myth of Arthur is all of myth by another name.

There are other allusions. Excalibur is a Celtic sword possessed of its *own* spirit – it was a strong belief that weapons contained elementals. Michael Moorcock's *Elric* stories are among the best contemporary fictional usages of that idea; and in one

remarkable Irish tale, a warrior's shield is so incensed by its owner's slackness in battle that it spins from his hand and severs his head from his body.

Excalibur is produced from water, by the Lady of the Lake – an echo of Brigga, Goddess of Rivers – water being a barrier between the real and the "other" world. It is to that Otherworld that the sword is returned, and across the water to Avalon that Arthur is taken, in a barge occupied entirely by women, one of whom is the "fay" Morgan. Repeatedly, the image of three women, or three queens, is encountered in the literature. Black clad, mournful, they are the three faces of the tri-partite goddess of ancient times: fecundity, motherhood and the hag of death. In the romances they are beautiful queens who control entry to the realm of healing.

Avalon. The Otherworld. It was known by many names, the Delightful Plain, the Land of Promise, the Many Coloured Land and so on. There was no hard and fast belief in either the "form" of the place, or the way of reaching the Otherworld, although two traditions are always strongly represented, and they almost certainly refer to a *very* ancient belief. The first is that Avalon is reached through an island, across water; the second is that it is reachable through a magic cave on a hillside, either a natural hill or the strange burial mounds that we call tumuli and which were associated with gateways to the land of a vanished folk more than four thousand years ago! The priests might know exactly how to pass from the mortal realm into the realm of the dead, but for most of the Britons, only the island or the hill could be seen.

If you were a Celt, this is how you might think of Avalon: "The Otherworld co-exists with our own. Sometimes the veil between the two worlds parts and the gods, and the dead, walk our land. This happens in winter especially, at the beginning of November in particular, and on that evening when the ghosts are free the gods must be appeased and protection against the supernatural taken. But the Otherworld is a joyous place to visit – and mortals *may* visit, although they may never return, because the music is so exquisite, the feasting endless, the hunting and the battles glorious. It is a world very like the real world, where the dead become immortal and ride and feast with the gods, paying attendance on the Lord of the Dead, who in some traditions is called Avallach. Avalon is Avallach's realm. When I die I shall be buried with my chariot and my weapons on the island that is the gate to Avalon. I will then rise and enter the Otherworld. I may, at some future time, return as a warrior, or as a sacred beast, half animal, half god."

Here, then, in the religious belief of perhaps three thousand years ago are the image-seeds of the romance recorded by the writers of the Age of Chivalry: the magic realm, reached by a water journey, entered through a concealed cave; the realm where death is unknown, and therefore mortal wounds are cured; the realm from which return is possible at some later age.

Avalon is the Delightful Plain, the Beautiful Valley. It co-exists with a part of our world, and we can never see it. But the gateways to Avalon are manifold and all around us. There are the giant tomb mounds of Ireland, the caves in the Glamorgan hills, the sea-caves on the Cornish coast, the great ring of stones at Stonehenge. Were any of them the gate that the dying Arthur took? The answer is almost certainly no. There is a gateway to Avalon of more dramatic and mystic nature than any of those places: the passage to Avalon for a King, or a tribal priest, a place with haunting echoes of the earliest gateway to the Delightful Plain.

The first Celtic peoples to migrate towards Britain, and perhaps settle here, had come originally from Switzerland. At Hallstatt the remains of the centre of a great community have been discovered, giving the name to this early Iron Age culture. The Hallstatt settlement is on the shore of a vast lake, looking towards the imposing rise of a mountain. On the slopes of that mountain, presided over by priests and priestesses, the noble dead were buried. They were rowed across the lake, with their weapons and their riches, and interred in "caves", from whence they journeyed to the fabulous realm.

By the time the first members of that culture were walking the ridgeways between the forests, to the North of England, and to the west – in the first millennium BC – the memory of that sacred mountain, gateway to Avalon, must have been haunting and precious. It is almost possible to hear the cries of astonishment when, one evening as the sun set above the mists of lake and marsh, the sharply rising Tor of Glastonbury appeared in the distance. The mountain at Hallstatt would have dwarfed it, but these travellers were generations removed from the sight of the jagged peaks of their homeland. They approached through a marshland that was eerie with fog and will-o-the-wisp, and echoed with the dusk cries of corncrakes, herons and pelicans. The Tor could be seen for miles, rising from an island of land, surrounded by water.

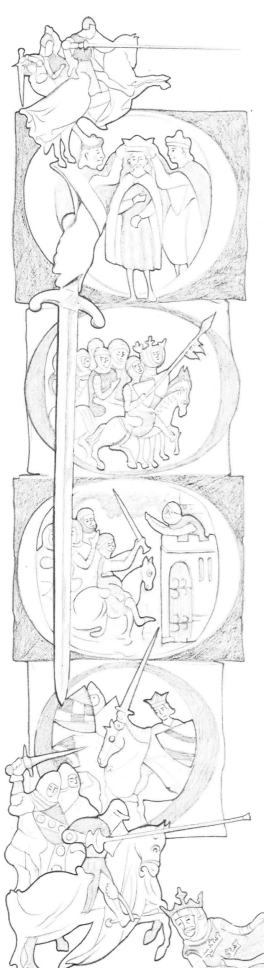

The earliest settlements at the hallowed site have gone, although the remains of the lake village of a later settlement have been excavated. But it is a haunting question to ask: somewhere upon the hill of Glastonbury, or in the now dry marshes around its base, are the corpses of generations of warchiefs, druids and princesses to be found, taken across the brackish water to the Otherworld?

What gateway to Avalon could have been more appropriate for the dead warlord Arthur? No matter where the site of the battle where he died, surely his corpse would have been carried by his surviving knights to the marshes and the much shrunken lake that bordered the Tor?
But according to the monk Nennius, Arthur had fought with the image of the Virgin Mary upon his shoulders. He had been raised in a country where the Christian faith was now the faith of Kings. His mentor, Ambrosius Aurelianus, was more Roman than Celt, and must surely have been of the faith of Christ.

So perhaps the body of Arthur was borne to Glastonbury not for the memory of the pagan Otherworld, but because already Glastonbury was a sanctified shrine of Christianity. Already, there were stories of Joseph of Arimethea having planted his staff where the new, tiny abbey was being built. Celtic Christian monks gathered at this place that had once been of such importance to their forebears. They celebrated the One God…but *surely* they were drawn to Glastonbury by the power of nature, of Cernunnos the Lord of Animals, of Brigga, of Epona, the huntress figure of Moon and Horse; and of all the mind-gods of the Iron Age.

Oddly, Arthur's burial at Glastonbury is not recorded in any of the sources that one might logically expect to have featured such an account. The monk Gildas, especially, is negligent on this point, not even mentioning Arthur at all. Perhaps the burial did not take place… And yet, centuries later, the association of Arthur and Glastonbury was sufficiently strong for the monks of the Norman monastery to dig for Arthur's grave and find a cross, buried centuries earlier, with Arthur's name upon it! If nothing else – and it is highly unlikely that the burial so discovered *was* that of Arthur – it reinforces first the use of the area as a place of ancient burial, and second, the association of man and place. Yet Gildas denies him.

Was there an early account of Arthur's death that was such anathema to the monks of Christian Britain that they struck it – and Arthur – from the records? Might that account – which remained available as a source of fact to several later writers, even though it is now lost to us – have been the mysterious *Book of the British*, often referred to, denied to modern readers by the destructiveness of ages?

And what, one wonders, did that *Book of the British* have to say of Arthur and his battles? Did it say that he formed a cavalry unit under the auspices not of the Virgin Mary, but of the moon goddess Epona, Queen of Horses, whose image is shown both as a woman and as a stylized horse, such as the chalk figure at Uffington, in Wiltshire? Did it say that Arthur rode the frontier between Celt and Saxon and inspired, in the minds of the clans, a memory of the great heroes and tales of their Celtic forebears, of Peredur, Owein, Bran the Mighty, Nuadd of the Silver Hand, and all the rest? Did Arthur manage, briefly, to forge a new pride in the fatherland of the Celts, a pride that Christianity had been eroding with its worship of an invisible Lord, who cared nothing for material things?

This was the land of our fathers. In *their* name, and in memory of the gods who watch us from Avalon, hold this land against the pagan!

And hold that land they did, for two generations or more. Arthur died in a civil war against his kinsman, Medraut. Charismatic leaders followed, probably Arthur's sons, but the Saxons were strong again, and the power of the Cross had weakened that briefly found Celtic pride. The real Dark Age was a storm of fire and pillage that appals the senses, and makes of the latter part of the sixth century a blight upon the land.

But what had the *Book of the British* to say of Arthur's death? Did it describe how his closest knights, Peredur and Kei among them, took Arthur's body secretly to the sacred Tor at Glastonbury, where his sister and two other women who were overseers of the shrine, rowed the dead warlord across the small lake, out of sight of the monastery? While the knights returned to battle, the sad women stripped the corpse of the king of its armour and weaponry, and buried these in a concealed passage on the slopes of the Tor. The corpse they interred on the top of the hill, and marked it with a stone. Later, a church was built upon the site, hiding the grave forever. But by that time Arthur had long since risen from the cold earth and stepped down the Tor, into the bright valley of Avalon.

It is said that Arthur waits for the call to return to the world of mortal humankind. But he has never, really, been away. Avalon is a place of the mind, a realm of belief and imagination. Arthur waits there, and waits, therefore, in all of us. His symbolic power is not that he reflects the glory and the romance of war, and honour, and spiritual renewal, rather that he links us with a past that has never gone away, and ties us to an earth that has changed very little.

He is not the Once and Future King; Arthur is the Once and Always Man.

lyonesse

The fair realm of Lyonesse lay a hundred and fifty miles west of the great forts at Cadbury, Badbury and Old Sarum, further west than the narrow peninsular of cliff and rock-strewn landscape which now is known as Land's End. It rose from the waters of the Atlantic, a great island, a place of deep, lush valleys and high, craggy hills upon which a hundred majestic castles had been built over the ages. Some even say that a narrow land bridge existed between Lyonesse and Cornwall.

Out of Lyonesse came the fairest and most noble of princesses to marry into the bloodlines of the Wessex and later Celtic Kings. From Lyonesse rode the most courageous and gallant of Arthur's knights, Sir Tristam and Sir Galahad among them. To Lyonesse those knights returned after the death of Arthur, at the field of Badon, and some legend says that Medraut's mercenaries pursued them, beyond St Michael's mount, off Land's End, almost to the borders of Lyonesse itself. A final stand of arms on the fair fields of this luxurious land, however, was prevented by the cataclysm that drowned Lyonesse forever. The land split open –

an earthquake which some say was induced by magic – and the seas poured in. One knight alone rode ahead of the great tidal wave and reached the safety of Cornwall. For the rest, they lay either drowned in their strongholds, or they rode furiously to the highest land of the realm, a place now known as the Scilly Isles. There they waited, and are waiting still, for Arthur to summon them to battle again.

What makes the various legends and myths of Lyonesse so fascinating is that some of the land area referred to in the stories *did* exist. Mid-way between the Scilly Isles and Land's End the sea bed rises dramatically, and from the reefs that graze the ocean's surface can be dredged the trunks of ancient trees, a testimonial to the forested land that is now drowned. At very low tide, man-made walls and field boundaries can be seen stretching out across the sand flats so exposed. A great island chain once stretched westwards from Cornwall, but the natural shift of the land caused all but the highest of them to be swallowed by the waves (as the lagoons of Kent, across the country, were raised up to form marshes).

In the myths of many nations, the West, the place of the setting sun, is a powerful story focus. Atlantis, one of the earliest images from legend, is a lost land in the west, and Lyonesse has often been called the "British Atlantis". This is hardly surprising as much of the "matter" of Atlantis has become incorporated into the Lyonesse story. And not just Atlantis; legends of the City of Ys have also become overlain upon that of Lyonesse. The City of Ys was a legendary Breton stronghold, rising from the sea off the western shores of Brittany, and lost under similar circumstances to its Cornish counterpart. Indeed, the myth of the City of Ys is quite likely to be the earlier, and the formative legend of both locations. How the stories of Ys arose is not hard to see. The coastline of Brittany is littered with the gigantic megalithic monuments and stone circles of the New Stone Age. At low tide, in some of the Brittany bays, weed-racked monolithic structures appear, like dark, glistening creatures, above the ebbing waters. No wonder there is a story cycle relating to a vanished land.

As with the legend of Arthur, a memory of a sunken, forested island in the western seas may have become associated and combined with many other myths and stories held in common belief. The link between Lyonesse and the Celtic Land Below the Waves is strong. The Land Below the Waves was a mystic and beautiful city that existed below the water, warmed always by the orange disc of the setting sun. Lyonesse is spoken of as a lush and beautiful place of incredible antiquity and may well have been thought of as an Otherworld as potent as Avalon.

In this way are legends made: first memory, then folk-lore, then a superstitious awe of almost religious intensity. Eventually it is the awesome aspect that remains, and the essential truth is gone...

A land of old, unheaven from the abyss
By fire to sink into the abyss again;
Where fragments of forgotten people dwelt
And the long mountains ended in a coast
Of ever-shifting sand, and far away
The phantom circle of a moaning sea...

The Passing of Arthur
Alfred, Lord Tennyson

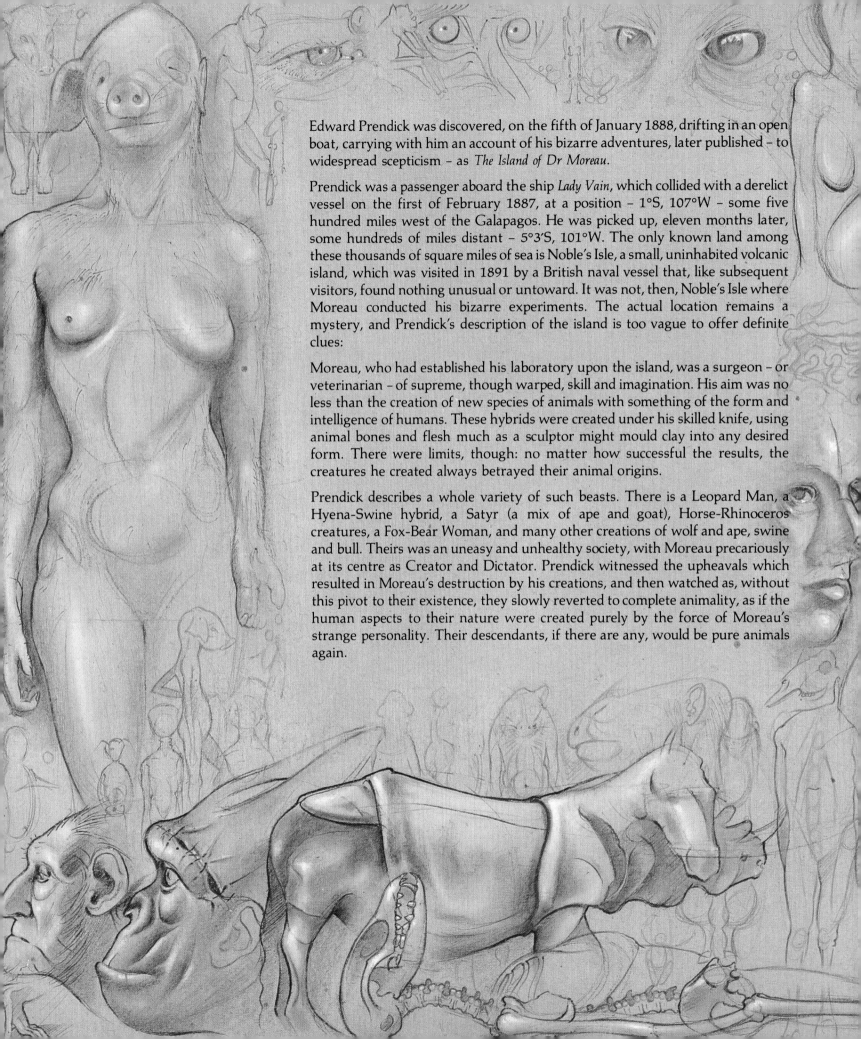

Edward Prendick was discovered, on the fifth of January 1888, drifting in an open boat, carrying with him an account of his bizarre adventures, later published – to widespread scepticism – as *The Island of Dr Moreau*.

Prendick was a passenger aboard the ship *Lady Vain*, which collided with a derelict vessel on the first of February 1887, at a position – 1°S, 107°W – some five hundred miles west of the Galapagos. He was picked up, eleven months later, some hundreds of miles distant – 5°3'S, 101°W. The only known land among these thousands of square miles of sea is Noble's Isle, a small, uninhabited volcanic island, which was visited in 1891 by a British naval vessel that, like subsequent visitors, found nothing unusual or untoward. It was not, then, Noble's Isle where Moreau conducted his bizarre experiments. The actual location remains a mystery, and Prendick's description of the island is too vague to offer definite clues:

Moreau, who had established his laboratory upon the island, was a surgeon – or veterinarian – of supreme, though warped, skill and imagination. His aim was no less than the creation of new species of animals with something of the form and intelligence of humans. These hybrids were created under his skilled knife, using animal bones and flesh much as a sculptor might mould clay into any desired form. There were limits, though: no matter how successful the results, the creatures he created always betrayed their animal origins.

Prendick describes a whole variety of such beasts. There is a Leopard Man, a Hyena-Swine hybrid, a Satyr (a mix of ape and goat), Horse-Rhinoceros creatures, a Fox-Bear Woman, and many other creations of wolf and ape, swine and bull. Theirs was an uneasy and unhealthy society, with Moreau precariously at its centre as Creator and Dictator. Prendick witnessed the upheavals which resulted in Moreau's destruction by his creations, and then watched as, without this pivot to their existence, they slowly reverted to complete animality, as if the human aspects to their nature were created purely by the force of Moreau's strange personality. Their descendants, if there are any, would be pure animals again.

ISLANDS

In the great era of exploration, ships set sail from England and Spain, Holland and Portugal, crossing and recrossing the oceans in search of wonderful new lands to explore and conquer. The sailors were men of great courage, navigating with the aid of inadequate charts, never knowing if any trip would prove to be their last. They travelled to the Americas, to the East Indies, across the Pacific Ocean – and later, to Australasia. Many of their destinations became important colonies, but others have, mysteriously, never been found again.

Many authors were inspired by sailors' accounts to write about islands which were either distorted versions of places they had heard about, or were imaginary lands in which they could set adventures, romances, or cautionary tales. Sometimes it is hard to tell which is which. Daniel Defoe's *Robinson Crusoe*, for instance, is one of the first great novels, but it is based on the true story of the marooned sailor Alexander Selkirk. It gave rise to entire genre of fiction, the "robinsonade", in which people cast ashore on strange lands struggle for survival. A fairly recent example is Jules Verne's *Mysterious Island*, in which a group of Americans crash their balloon on a strange desert island where odd creatures are to be found, but endure to build a miniature industrial society of their own.

Another celebrated imaginary or vanished island, which gave rise to another tradition, was Utopia, described by Thomas More in 1516 in his famous work of the same name. Utopia, supposedly discovered by a Portuguese sailor called Raphael Hythloday (who had journeyed to the Americas with Vespucci), was an apparently perfect society, harmonious and peaceful, run by its citizens in a democratic way (though there is also slavery), free of the corruption which tainted European society.

Other writers described utopian states supposedly found on other islands. Erewhon, written about by Samuel Butler, was an island somewhere in the vicinity of New Zealand, where machines were banned because of fears that they might evolve and supplant the human race. Butler uses his narrative to comment on Victorian society in England, notably as satire on religion.

Perhaps the most detailed imaginary island is Islandia, to the description of which the American Austin Tappan Wright – 1883-1931 – devoted much of his adult life. Islandia was a utopian society situated somewhere in the vicinity of the Antarctic, and Wright described its history, geography and culture in enormous detail. Eleven years after his death a book was published, titled *Islandia*, but although it was more than a thousand pages long it constituted only a tiny fraction of the material. To give just one example, Wright's papers included a monograph on Islandia, supposedly written by a French visitor to the island, which alone was 135,000 words in length. Islandia was, in fact, more fully documented than many islands which are to be found on modern maps, and in that sense is no less real.

In 1726 was published a book entitled *Travels into Several Remote Nations of the World*, whose author described himself as "Lemuel Gulliver, first a Surgeon, and then a Captain of Several Ships". Gulliver spent the early part of the eighteenth century on a number of long sea voyages to parts of the world then unexplored, and brought back extraordinary accounts of his adventures, which became immediate best-sellers. The stories do appear far-fetched, and although Gulliver provided maps showing the locations of the strange lands he discovered, none of them has ever been found by subsequent travellers.

Lilliput and its neighbouring island Blefescu, were the scene of Gulliver's first adventure. Situated some hundreds of miles south-west of Sumatra, they are small islands which nevertheless maintained large populations because of a curious circumstance: none of the inhabitants were more than 6 inches high. To the Lilliputians, of course, Gulliver was a giant (he was dubbed the Man-Mountain). The capital of Lilliput was the city of Mildendo, which Gulliver describes in some detail: it is a square, five hundred feet long on each side, within which lives a population of half a million people. The walls are two and a half feet high and eleven inches thick. Two great thoroughfares, each five inches wide, divide the city into quarters. The Emperor's palace, a building of magnificence, is housed within gardens forty feet square at the intersection of these roads. Gulliver promises further description of the city and the remainder of the kingdom in a larger work "now almost ready for the press", but that book was never published and now, like Lilliput itself, is lost.

While Gulliver was in Lilliput the kingdom was at war, as it had been for many years, with neighbouring Blefescu. Like many long-running disputes, a religious schism lay at the core of the conflict; in this instance, it was about the correct way to crack open a boiled egg – whether at the Little End, as prescribed by religious orthodoxy and observed in Lilliput; or, heretically, at the Big End, as practised by the Blefescans.

Gulliver's second destination was Brobdingnag, and here it is clear that he – at the very least – exaggerates grossly, for he speaks of a land six thousand miles long and three thousand miles wide and one which, moreover, is not an island but a peninsula, attached to the north-west coast of America – near what is now Vancouver – by a narrow, mountainous isthmus. Here dwell a race of giants, some hundred and fifty feet tall, cut off from maritime commerce by their mountainous shoreline. There are fifty-one cities and about a hundred walled towns. Gulliver describes only the capital. Lorbrulgrud, which is situated along a river bank, and is fifty-four miles long and two and a half miles broad. This vast metropolis houses some two hundred thousand giants. The palace of the King is not a stately edifice, but is rather a haphazard aggregation of buildings with a perimeter of seven miles. The Brobdingnagians were peaceful and civilized people, appalled by Gulliver's accounts of European life.

The most remarkable, however, of all the strange realms visited by Gulliver was Laputa. It lay somewhere to the east of Japan, in the vicinity of the island of Balnibarbi – indeed, sometimes at precisely the same location as Balnibarbi, because Laputa was a *flying* island. It was perfectly circular, and some four and a half miles in diameter. Its base was a solid plate of adamant two hundred yards thick. The island was controlled by an immense magnet carefully mounted at its centre. By turning the magnet this way and that the island could be made to rise and fall and move laterally, according to the degree to which it was repelled by or attracted to the Earth.

The King of Laputa ruled over the Balnibarbians, stopping his island here and there to receive tribute (which was pulled aboard the island on thousands of hand-held winches resembling fishing tackle). There was little chance of revolt, since the King could simply position the island to hover over a recalcitrant settlement, cutting out all sunlight, until they saw the error of their ways. Stones might also be dropped on them, and there was an ultimate sanction – that of dropping the whole *island* on their heads, crushing them completely. Like many ultimate deterrents, though, this was not used, since some Laputans calculated that the impact might destroy the island as well as its intended victims.

Some of the most weird and wonderful lost islands are those which are mentioned in the voyages of Sinbad the merchant sailor. The tales form a part of the *One Thousand Nights and a Night* and date from a time when Baghdad and Basrah, in the lands we know of as Iraq, were at the peak of their trading prosperity. Merchants travelled to the China Seas and to the Baltic, carrying silks, jewels, metals and spices.

We know of only seven voyages that Sinbad made, each a moral fable that says if you are courageous and have integrity then no matter how bad you are at sailing you will get wealthy in Allah's name. Seven voyages have come down to us, but there is rumour of an eighth adventure, believed to have survived in a strange parchment and baldly entitled *The Forbidden Voyage*.

By the Will of Allah, and the Grace of God, I returned to the sea in the fiftieth year of my life. A favourable wind carried me south for many days, towards the Black Isle, and on the way I traded from island to island.

In this uncertain eighth journey Sinbad is actually *questing*, searching for a magical box which lies hidden upon the mountainside of the Black Isle. As he approaches the Isle the usual disaster occurs.

Suddenly a strange wind tugged at the ship and upon all who sailed her. All things metal were wrenched from their holdings and flung to the dark slopes of the huge island. There were those who lost the gold from their teeth, the buckles from their belts, the swords from their scabbards. All flew as if by magic across the waves to the glittering mountains. And the ship too was dragged to the rocks, with its cargo of pots, pans and weaponry pressed hard against the hull.

The island, it seems, is a gigantic magnet that attracts all metals, and the slopes gleam and glitter with the bones of men, still trapped in their armour. It is a wasteland of metal and precious objects. Swords and lances stand like bristles all across it. The metal hulks of strange ships rust among the ruins. And lost among this jetsam is the Casket.

The mountain slopes, however, are guarded by beast-like creatures that live in buildings made from the wreckage of ships and the bones of men. Sinbad fights with them and wins the right to search out the magic Casket, which he finds and opens. What is inside? All that is suggested by the fragment of manuscript is that he discovers a miniature ocean and a miniature ship which he somehow summons to take him home. The true secret of the casket is not revealed, nor is the location of the Black Isle.

The most recent lost island to be recorded is Skull Island, although its exact whereabouts remain uncertain – perhaps classified. It is situated somewhere in the Flores Sea, east of Java, an area of treacherous seas and myriad tiny landmasses. Skull Island escaped detection for centuries because of unusual meteorological and geological conditions, as a result of which it has remained hidden behind a perpetual shroud of heavy cloud and sea fog. Even aerial photography failed, at first, to pinpoint its location.

Isolated, cut off from the mainland for millions of years, Skull Island is one of those places where evolution has taken its own course, where creatures otherwise extinct still survive, and where developments unmatched on the mainland have occurred. What marks out the island is, of course, the exceptionally dramatic nature of these survivals and developments.

This island was first explored in 1930 by Carl Denham, Captain of an American expeditionary vessel. They were at first excited by the momentous discovery of a lost tribe, the Skull Islanders, as cut off and unknown as the Tasaday people in the Philippine jungles. Such a find would, by itself, have made headline news among anthropologists, but there was more – much more – to come.

The islanders confined themselves to the southwest tip of Skull Island, a flat and fertile area in which they raised a variety of crops and animals. The remainder of the island – though only a matter of some fifty square miles in area – was a dramatic wilderness, with a pair of tall mountain peaks – which may once have been part of a single great volcano, riven by an ancient eruption – surrounded by dense rain forest. The country was made even more difficult by fast-running rivers, deep gorges and precipitous cliffs. The islanders cut themselves off from this primeval terrain by building a huge wall, consisting of immense treetrunks lashed together with vines, their tops sharpened to form a gigantic stockade. This was, by itself, an impressive feat of primitive engineering, and at first Denham and his crew thought it served some religious and symbolic function – a Stonehenge of the East Indies.

But they soon discovered that the purpose of the wall was not symbolic but eminently practical. For in the deep forests of Skull Island roamed a number of creatures long believed extinct, and others never known to exist. There were dinosaurs – iguanodon, allosaurus, triceratops, pteranodon and others, left over from the Mesozoic Era, millions of years in the past. Most of these, despite their huge size, were herbivores, and thus of no threat to the islanders except through their huge size and uncertain temper. But others were among the largest and most vicious meat-eating animals our world has ever seen.

Tremendous though this discovery was, it was not unique – other enclaves of dinosaurs have been found in isolated parts of South America. What *was* unique to Skull Island was the creature now known to the scientific community as *gorilla giganticus*, or Denham's ape, but known to the world by the name given it by the Skull Islanders – Kong! Growing some fifty feet in height, Kong was the creature whom the Skull Islanders both worshipped and protected themselves against. Of course, there was more than one Kong – though the size of the colony has never been determined – but to the Islanders they were all one creature, or God. They placated Kong by offering sacrifices, and in return Kong left their little corner of the island alone. The gates in their stockade, however, being of a size to admit the great gorilla, suggest that in some rituals – as yet unknown – Kong was permitted to enter the Skull Islanders' village. As we now know, the attempt by the islanders to offer Ann Darrow, a member of Denham's crew, as a sacrifice to their God, led to the capture and, later, display, of one of the creatures. The tragic result of that misconceived piece of showmanship has led to a renewed cloak of quarantined secrecy being placed around this unique site.

But where are these islands? Perhaps their whereabouts were misrecorded. That happened commonly enough. Pitcairn Island, where the mutineers from the *Bounty* took refuge, remained a safe haven because it was misplaced by a hundred miles on the charts of the British Navy, thus being effectively lost in the vastness of the South Pacific. Now that Earth's seas have been surveyed by countless ships, observed and photographed from the air and from space, it seems improbable that there could still be forgotten specks of land – but there is a great gulf between the improbable and the impossible, and to claim that such places can *not* exist is to invite contradiction. If so, there may be marvels to be discovered, for on these lost islands – if they existed, and were not concocted by the feverish imaginations of sailors too long away from home – there were strange and wonderful sights to see and peoples to meet.

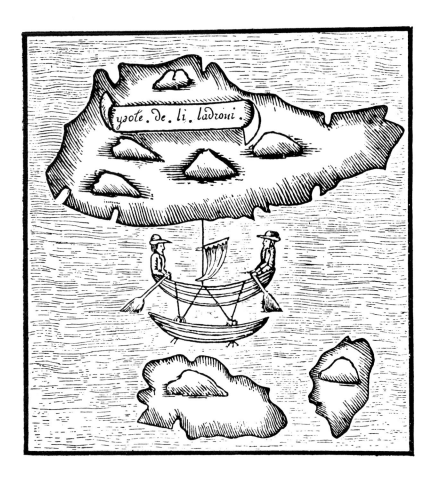

Continents

There are various theories to explain how the shape of continents has changed over the millennia. The two most important are the theory of cataclysmic rise and fall, and the theory of continental drift.

It is the latter which today is favoured by most scientists. According to the theory the Earth's crust is not solid, but is composed of a number of different "plates" which slide around extremely slowly, changing the configuration of the surface. It is the friction as the edges of these plates rub against and over each other that causes earthquakes.

Onc can see by looking closely at a world map how by distorting slightly the shape of present-day continents they can be pushed together into one huge primeval landmass – South America fitting neatly into the western curve of Africa and so forth. This original continent is sometimes known as Gondwanaland or Pangaea, but there are few legends to tell us about what life might have been like if such a place existed.

On the contrary, the legends all fit the former theory, that continents rise and fall as a result of so-far unexplained upheavals in the Earth's crust. These seem to happen quickly and cataclysmically, like an enormous earthquake pulverizing an entire continent. The Biblical tale of the Flood may result from such an event, since enormous tidal waves and climatic changes would result from it. Best known of all lost continents is, of course, Atlantis, described by many writers from Plato onwards and located somewhere across the Mediterranean and Atlantic. According to some writers the Atlanteans had a powerful civilization with many scientific wonders we still do not understand. This chapter looks in detail at some other accounts of vanished continents.

Tolkein's Númenor is the product of his prodigiously detailed imagination, but because it is built on his immense knowledge of legend and myth it is consistent with Biblical, classical and many other tales. It may be that in this fiction Tolkein has arrived at a synthesis that in some respects reconstructs history more accurately than other attempts not presented as fiction; his is a kind of *ur*-myth, a basic core from which many tales in many traditions could plausibly spring.

In the days before recorded history, as told by J. R. R. Tolkien in *The Lord of the Rings* and *The Silmarillion*, the gods still dwelt upon the Earth, and in addition to men there were elves and dwarves and other species. Most mortals lived on the great landmass of Middle-earth, while far to the west was the land of the Valar – the Guardians of the World – and the Eldar, those who had passed from Middle-earth into the Uttermost West and were now immortal.

The First Age of men upon Earth culminated in a great battle against the evil Morgoth, who eventually was overthrown. As a reward for all their suffering in this great conflict the Valar created a new land in which the men of the Edain could live. It was not part of either Middle-earth or Valinor, home of the Valar, and was separated from each by a wide stretch of sea, though it lay closer to Valinor. It was raised from the ocean depths and made fertile and fruitful, and was named Andor, the Land of Gift.

Guided by a star set in the sky by the Valar, the Edain set sail from Middle-earth and came to Andor, to which they gave many names, of which the best remembered is Númenor. They founded great cities, among them Andúnië, a haven which lay in the west; and Armenelos, the most beautiful of their cities, which was sited at the foot of a great mountain, the Meneltarma, or "Pillar of Heaven". At its summit was an open temple – the only temple in Númenor – from which the farsighted could envision the white tower of the Haven of the Eldar on the Isle of Eressëa, the easternmost of the immortal islands.

Assisted by gifts from the Eldar, the Númenoreans built a great and peaceful civilization, distinguished not least by their feats of seafaring. But there was one ban laid upon them in return for the gift of their land: they were forbidden to sail out of sight of Númenor to the west, though they could roam as they pleased in other directions. The purpose of this "Ban of the Valar" was to keep them from becoming tempted by the idea of immortal life, which they might think theirs if they sailed to Valinor.

For centuries the Númenoreans flourished, while Middle-earth itself was sinking into a dark age with the rise of Morgoth's former servant, Sauron. But envy of the Valar and the Eldar in time began to gnaw at them, though they did not break the ban, and they became obsessed with death and filled their land with great mausoleums in which the dead were embalmed and preserved. They sailed east to Middle-earth and built cities there and demanded tribute.

In time the power of Sauron came into conflict with that of Númenor, under the last of its kings, Ar-Pharazôn, and Sauron saw that Númenor was too mighty to defeat in battle. He allowed himself to be taken as a captive to Númenor. But in this moment of victory lay Ar-Pharazôn's defeat, and that of Númenor, for Sauron was cunning and devious and soon corrupted the king, telling him that the only purpose of the Ban of Valar was to keep the Kings of Men from possessing the Undying Lands – and their gift of immortality – for themselves. Sauron was soon free, and built an immense temple in the heart of Armenelos. It was a circular building, five hundred feet in diameter and five hundred feet tall. Its walls were fifty feet thick and it was roofed with a dome of silver. Here the worship of the dark god Melkor was followed, and Númenor became a place of fear and hatred, ruled over in name by Ar-Pharazôn, but in fact by Sauron.

As he grew old and afraid of death, Ar-Pharazôn began to plan the conquest of Valinor, and assembled the greatest fleet ever seen. The Valar gave warning in the form of storms and lightning and great rumblings of the earth, but Sauron's power was enough to deflect some of their portents, and the fleet sailed, led by Ar-Pharazôn in his great ship *Alcarondas*, the Castle of the Sea. Darkness fell over the world, and remained. Ar-Pharazôn in time arrived at the coast of Valinor, and almost turned back; but his pride got the better of him and he disembarked and claimed the land as his own.

Then the gods acted. They opened a great chasm in the sea, into which the waters poured. The Númenorean fleet was drawn into these immense cataracts and was lost. Ar-Pharazôn and others who had set foot upon Valinor were buried under falling hills. And Númenor itself was utterly destroyed. Its foundations were shattered and it collapsed into the sea from which it was raised, and was never seen again. The only survivors were the few who had remained faithful to the Valar, led by Elendil. In nine ships they sailed to Middle-earth, where they founded the kingdoms of Arnor and Gondor. Sauron was destroyed in his physical form; but his spirit took flight to Middle-earth and his land of Mordor,

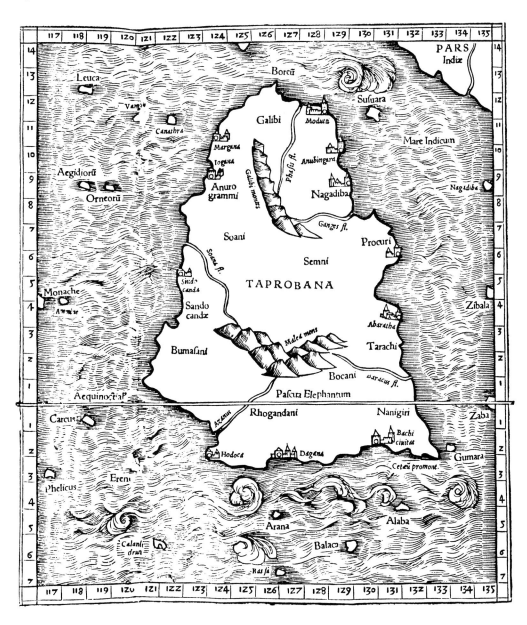

where he once again began to plot the downfall of his enemies.

Some said that the summit of Meneltarma, which had never been desecrated by Sauron, still survives – a tiny lonely isle in the midst of immense seas. But Númenor is gone. Even its name has been forgotten, and instead it is known as the Downfallen, the Akallabêth.

According to theories developed in the nineteenth century Lemuria is one of the oldest of lost continents, predating Atlantis. It is also one on which the human race had its origins.

The name "Lemuria" means "land of the lemurs", and it was coined because the idea of the ancient continent arose out of an attempt to explain the otherwise peculiar distribution of lemurs. These small monkey-like creatures (zoologically different from any other species) are to be found in large numbers on the island of Madagascar, and also in certain areas of Africa, India and Malaya. How to account for these odd enclaves of what are clearly closely-related species? One obvious idea is that at one time all these areas were joined as part of a vanished landmass encompassing much of the Indian and Pacific Oceans. This notion was put forward in the 1850s, notably by a German advocate of Darwinian theories, Ernst Haeckel. The name "Lemuria" was suggested by English zoologist Philip Sclater.

Once the idea had been advanced by zoologists, geologists were quick to allow that such a landmass might have existed. But a picture of what Lemuria might have been like did not arrive until the 1880s with the remarkable writings of Madame Helena Blavatsky, founder of the occult discipline of theosophy. Madame Blavatsky claimed to be in contact with a group of Mahatmas who lived somewhere in Tibet and had access to ancient wisdom through a work called the *Book of Dzyan*. The revelations it contained formed part of the basis of her own magnum opus, which she titled *The Secret Doctrine*. This revealed that modern *homo sapiens* is the fifth of seven Root Races – stages through which intelligent life evolves on its way to a state of grace. The first Root Race was almost protoplasmic. The Second, slightly more human, lived in the lost arctic continent of Hyperborea. The Fourth, fully human in their appearance, were the Atlanteans. The Third were the strange, half-human Lemurians. They were apelike in appearance, and were egg-laying hermaphrodites. Some of them had four arms, and others possessed a third eye in the back of their head.

These initial revelations were greatly developed by another Theosophist, W. Scott-Elliot, who pinned down the era of the Lemurians much more exactly. It coincided with the Mesozoic period, which we know primarily as the age of dinosaurs.

Scott-Elliot's occult sources enabled him to describe the Lemurians with some precision. They were between twelve and fifteen feet tall and brown-skinned.

They had rather apelike faces, with eyes set so far apart that they could see sideways as well as forwards. They had a third eye in the back of their heads, where the pineal gland is located in modern humans – the gland being a vestigial remnant. They could not completely straighten their limbs. A typical Lemurian would be dressed in a robe of reptile skin, would be armed with a wooden spear, and might lead around a pet dinosaur on a leash! This may all sound far-fetched, but years after Scott-Elliot published his vision of Lemuria, bones were found in south-east Asia of enormous fossil ape-men, corresponding in several particulars to his descriptions.

The Lemurians went through several stages of evolution – or Sub-Races – ceasing along the way to be hermaphrodites and learning to bear live young. At some point they were, it is said, contacted by beings from another world, possibly Venus, who were known as the "Lords of the Flame". These powerful beings taught the Lemurians to lengthen their lifespan and instructed them in many crafts.

In time, great continental shifts again began to take place. Lemuria broke up as various parts sank beneath the encroaching seas, while at the same time Atlantis began to rise in the North Atlantic. The first Sub-Race of the Atlanteans were the last of the Lemurians, the Rmoahals. They were dark-skinned people, ten or twelve feet tall, who settled the southern coast of the new continent.

Lemuria might have been thought to have gone forever, but as recently as the 1930s serious reports were published in the USA of people claiming to have encountered a last colony of surviving Lemurians living a peaceful existence in the wilderness around Mount Shasta in Northern California. Their sacred village was forbidden to outsiders, and nobody could penetrate its intangible defences, but one scientist – Professor Edgar Larkin – did claim to have spied on it by telescope. He saw, in the heart of their community, a beautiful temple of carved marble and onyx, similar in style and magnificence to the great temples of the Aztecs and Maya. The surviving Lemurians no longer had eyes in the backs of their heads, or any of the other peculiarities described by Scott-Elliot. Instead they were tall, noble-looking people who dressed in white robes. They were supposedly possessors of scientific knowledge far in advance of our own, which included the ability to erect an invisible barrier around their home, and also the capacity to make themselves invisible to ordinary humans, perhaps through hypnosis. They still remembered their ancestral home, and commemorated it each night by illuminating Mount Shasta with red and green light.

There is no doubt that Madame Blavatsky, Scott-Elliot and the other Theosophists were quite serious in their beliefs, and that they produced a mass of detail in support of their version of our pre-history. Scott-Elliot even had maps and globes of the Lemurian and Atlantean worlds, whose details had been revealed to him by mystic contacts. Today, Theosophy is viewed as an interesting but cranky cult of the late nineteenth century by most rationalists, but occultists in many cases still accept its revelations, and with them the story of Lemuria. As for the Lemurians of Mount Shasta, they have today hidden themselves much more effectively from human eyes. Nobody has claimed to see them in the last half-century.

The lost continent of Mu, which in some respects may correspond to either Atlantis or Lemuria, was first identified in 1896 by a French-American physicist Dr Auguste La Plongeon. His researches into Mayan writings led him to deduce the existence of the place, which he placed somewhere adjacent with Central America and which he identified as the *real* Atlantis. The theory was developed, however, by Colonel James Churchward, who in 1926 published a popular book titled *The Lost Continent of Mu*, which was followed by several further works.

Churchward had, he tells us, learned details of the place from tablets of ancient writing discovered in Central America and in India (where he was taught how to decipher them). They revealed that Mu was in fact in the Pacific, stretching Hawaii to Fiji, and from East Island to the Marianas. Its shape was like an enormously enlarged New Guinea. Mu was flat, covered in tropical vegetation. At its height Mu had a population of sixty-four million people, who were divided into ten tribes and ruled over by a king called the Ra. The dominant race was white, though the people of Mu came in all colours.

According to Churchward there are gas-belts underneath the Earth's crust – huge caves filled with explosive gas mixtures, perhaps like the methane sometimes encountered by miners. The destruction of Mu was the result of a cataclysmic explosion in one of these caves, which caused it to collapse. Mu was shaken by huge earthquakes, then consumed by enormous gouts of flame, some of them three miles in diameter. All the cities and almost all the people were destroyed as the remnants of the land sank beneath the waves. All that was left was a scattering of islands, some of them bearing mysterious relics – such as the statues of Easter Island. The few survivors were so traumatized by the experience that they soon reverted to savagery and forgot their origins. The only clues left were a handful of tablets and fragments of manuscript, which Churchward was able to decipher to give a picture of Mu as it was. Regrettably, other scholars have been unable to view these sources in order to refute or confirm his theories.

Lemuria and Mu are both continents which have been supposed to exist by many serious people, although today such speculations tend to be dismissed as pseudoscience. It is difficult to believe in them very strongly, because the people who have described them would not make available their evidence for independent scientific verification. This tends to lead to the assumption that there is no such evidence, but that cannot be proved either. They may have had other reasons. Individual belief in the existence and nature of these lost continents must be determined by individual assessment of their plausibility. Nevertheless, it seems unlikely that there was not *some* great catastrophe in ancient history that would account for the persistence of such stories.

CITIES

When were the first cities built? And where? Were they, perhaps, in the rich river valleys of the Tigris and the Euphrates, the classical location of Eden and the so-called "cradle of mankind"? Or were the first cities to be found in East Africa, the place where, by all accounts, the first men developed? What a rich body of legend comes down to us from East Africa, partly because of its remoteness until very recently, and partly because of its fanciful association with the Queen of Sheba and Egypt, and the legend of lost "white" tribes and huge, beautiful cities within the high mountains.

When we think of cities we think of sprawling metropoli, but the first city would have been the largest of a group of towns, a defended place, a central place, a place of government for a wide rural population. With walls of mud-brick, or sandstone, the earliest great cities were almost extensions of the earth itself, and it is to the earth that they have returned. The stone walls of Zimbabwe, in Southern Africa, remained, sun-baked and high, awaiting "discovery" in 1871 by Karl Mauch. Mauch's find began a stream of fanciful conjecture about the place: that it was the fabled city of Ophir from which Solomon had brought a fabulous treasure back to Israel; that the Queen of Sheba had built it – anything and everything rather than acknowledge its construction by the local tribes peoples in the fourteenth century. Zimbabwe has remained standing, but the walls of Uruk, the great city of Sumeria built before 3000 BC, one of the homes of the earliest writing and the home of the first of all great Arthurian-type heroes, Gilgamesh, vanished below the dust and sand, to be rediscovered by Leonard Woolley. In the Southern continent of America dense rain forests grow over the great stone terraces and walls of the Inca and Aztec cities, hiding the masonry, hiding the gold... From the air there is just jungle. Nature, either by growth or the shifting of soil, obliterates the works of man in just a few decades. Unlike those islands and continents which are lost by catastrophe, cities become lost because of the steady passage of time and the gentle reclamation by the earth itself.

Sometimes they are lost simply by being abandoned: the city and site of the battle of Alesia in France, where Julius Caesar defeated the Gauls under Vercingetorix in 55 BC, was forgotten through shame, and remains a mystery to this day. And where is Camelot? Where is the stronghold of Arthur and his knights? Perhaps, as Leslie Alcock believes, it is to be found only in the dim memory of the great fortifications and earth ramparts of the huge hill fort of Cadbury, in Somerset.

Ancient and legendary cities excite the imagination because of their association, not so much with the grain that would have been stored in them, but with the gold that was hidden in the vaults of their treasuries; not so much with the mercantile aspect of their everyday lives as with the glory of the wars of defence and honour that were fought about their walls. Real or imaginary, such cities live longest in the public mind. And perhaps the classic example is that of Troy, a mythological city of Greek romance, suddenly discovered as being real. In Homer's epic poem the *Iliad* Troy is described as a great city state, opposed to the power that was Athens. A war of retribution in the second millennium BC, the launching of a thousand ships, the trick of the wooden horse, the death of Hector and Achilles, the burning of Troy to avenge the stealing of Helen... What stirring stuff Homer wrote! But did Troy exist? For hundreds of years it was believed that Troy was a fiction, an amalgam of many cities, the *Iliad* a mere story drawing upon the conflicts between city states in the Mediterranean world of the second millennium. But the German archaeologist Heinrich Schliemann believed that Troy *had* existed, and in the 1880s, and using the *Iliad* as a sort of guide book, he traced the site to the *tell* (artificial mound) of Hissarlik, in modern Turkey. The story thereafter is familiar. Schliemann found not just one Troy, but *nine* successive cities dating from 3000 BC to the final fall in Roman times. He also found buried gold – much of which he smuggled from the site beneath his wife's skirts, to preserve it from the corrupt local officials – and clear evidence of the burning of the city that had existed at the time of Homer's *Iliad*. The *Iliad* is therefore history, written with an eye for a good story. After four thousand years, Troy surfaced from the earth again.

The lost city of Troy excites because of its association with gold and glory. But cities excite, too, because they are foci of wisdom, the places of learning and the storehouses of that understanding and world consciousness. When Alexandria burned by Roman fire, a treasurehouse of documents, books and esoteric knowledge was totally lost – or was it? It is not just that manuscripts might still survive in lost or hidden vaults below the modern city, but that that same knowledge might survive in a city elsewhere – perhaps Shambhala. Shambhala? Since James Hilton wrote his classic novel, *Lost Horizon*, Shambhala is more familiarly known as Shangri-la. It is not the name that matters, but the myth.

In a seventeenth century Russian tradition it is known as Belovodye. It is believed to lie north of Tibet, in the remote and impenetrable snow wastes and mountains of what is now Southern Russia. It is believed to be the city from which an Ancient Wisdom originated. Evidence for its existence grows stronger.

Shambhala means "peace". Belovodye means "white waters". It is the place beyond the north wind, the mythical homeland of the Hyperboreans, the race who spread east, south and west from that homeland and shaped much of Europe and the near East as we know it, basing their cults and culture on the Ancient Wisdom.

Central to the Ancient Wisdom – if one accepts there having ever been such a thing – is the number seven. Seven is a lucky number, of course, but for decades, even centuries, its importance in religious tradition (from Celtic Ireland to Hindustan) has been acknowledged. There are seven pillars of wisdom, seven deadly sins, seven virtues, seven ages of man, seven notes in the musical scale, from A to G, seven wonders of the world, seven days of the week, seven gates to the Greek Hades, seven steps on Babylon's ziggurat, seven walls around Sumerian cities, seven twists in one of the most ancient and potent symbols of all, the labyrinth. This is commonly – and narrowly – associated with the Minotaur, but Glastonbury Tor is ridged around in the labyrinth pattern, and it is even found among the Hopi Indians of Arizona.

Seven moving objects in the sky – five planets, the moon and the sun – were noted by ancient observers, and seven stars in the brightest constellation, Ursa Major – linked with a bear since the third millennium if not earlier. And perhaps, as a result of this, the Ancient Wisdom may have been the first wisdom that reflected "As above, so below". It was the first insight into a link between the vast and the minute, between celestial bodies and the components of terrestrial matter. An understanding, a deep perception as regards pattern, organisation and influence – even gravity! – may have developed in the remote, philosophically orientated centre in the high mountains. It was a wisdom that disseminated in all directions: to India, to the Mediterranean, to western Europe; a knowledge which changed, was modified and adapted, but which is still expressively visible when the myth is stripped away. Druid and Guru, dreamstate and meditation, stone circle and mandala, Olympian god and force of nature, magic mountain and land below the hills, all, cryptically, speak of the same first insight, the insight that said our earth is part of a pattern that is more vast than one mind can imagine.

But where *was* Shambhala? To the early Hindus it was a high and paradisal place, located on the World Mountain, Meru. On Meru lived the seven Rishis, or sages, and their wisdom was all-pervading. Meru linked heaven and earth and was, by tradition, thought of in the North. The Sumerians, too, write of a mountain of heaven and earth which was the home of the gods. The Greeks brought the mountain closer to home – Olympus – but they never lost belief in a northern paradise "at the back of the north wind", the home of the semi-deified Hyperboreans. From that realm came the god Apollo, who journeyed between Olympus and the northern paradise and thus reflected the link between "a higher place and a lower place". His female companion, Artemis, also a Hyperborean, had Ursa Major as her celestial sign, and both gods had attributes measurable in "seven". The biblical writer Ezekiel, too, can still be seen to have a concept of a holy mountain in the far north, which is a paradise and heavenly place. Often linked with Mount Zion, in Palestine, there are hints that Ezekiel is referring to something much more remote when he sees Yahweh's fiery chariot hurtling towards him on a storm wind, from a high place in the north that is *not* the direction of the holy mountain of the Bible lands.

Combined with the European tradition is the Asian tradition already referred to, the Mongolian Chang Shambhala, the northern place of peace, identifiable as Belovodye, White Waters, which to the Russians was a lost valley in the east – from their vantage point – and a paradise. Modern tradition places it in Tibet, but reading between the lines the original location was far less accessible – in the Altai mountains, a vast range of peaks stretching from Siberia into north-western Mongolia.

From Chang Shambhala came the teaching known, to Lamaistic Bhuddists, as the Wheel of Time. To the Lamas, only the pure in thought can find the obscure secret route through the clustered mountains, to the cave and narrow defile that leads to the enclosed valley with its paradisal garden and city. To the Lamas, too, Chang Shambhala is not only the source of an older wisdom, but a lively and active centre of philosophy to this day. This may be taking belief into the realm of whimsy, although not to the degree that is expressed by those who see, in the astronomical connections between Shambhala and the stars, in the visions of fiery chariots appearing from the north, and Apollo riding his sky chariot to the high land beyond the wind, evidence for a more alien nature to the mythical city. Shambhala is associated with flying saucers, with the appearance of thought-created forms (of men, animals and indeed flying objects) and immortality. It is as if the need for there *still* to be a strange and esoteric knowledge lost in those mountain fastnesses is as strong as the need to find the lost world itself, and imagination continues to impose mysticism upon what may be no more than a snow-concealed ruin.

Eldorado, the golden city, hidden somewhere in the vast interior of South America – this is one of the most potent and enduring legends of lost realms. For more than a hundred years, from the beginning of the sixteenth century, the story obsessed European adventurers, who mounted expedition after failed expedition in search of the city and its fabulous riches. Some of them returned with great wealth in gold and emeralds; many more of them did not return at all; none of them found the place they were seeking.

After a time the adventurers began to go elsewhere in search of easy riches – to Africa, and to the East Indies. Yet the legend of Eldorado endured and grew, until the name became a synonym for anything greatly desirable yet unattainable. Even today the story endures – because even today large tracts of the South American hinterland remain unexplored by anyone except the Indian natives, and who knows what relics of lost civilizations might yet remain concealed among the jungles and rain forests?

The story of Eldorado – more properly two words, El Dorado – began with the arrival of the Spanish *conquistadores* in Central and South America in the early part of the sixteenth century. Here they discovered several powerful and ancient civilizations, strange and barbarous to European eyes. In Mexico and Central America were the empires of the Aztecs and the Maya, and other lesser nations; in Peru was the vast realm of the Incas. Although the Aztecs and Incas knew nothing of each other's existence, their empires had certain features in common. Their architectural skills were formidable, in their differing styles: the Inca cities with their great walls of irregular polished stone, fitted so closely that it is impossible to insert a knifeblade at any point; the Aztec and Maya temples, huge stepped pyramids of expertly dressed stone. The Aztecs, with their human sacrifices – cutting the heart from the living, yet willing, victim – seemed the more savage, though the Inca God-King held a more complete power of life and death over his subjects.

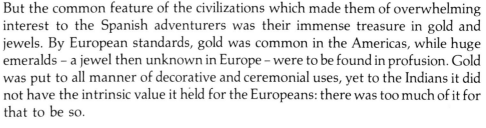

But the common feature of the civilizations which made them of overwhelming interest to the Spanish adventurers was their immense treasure in gold and jewels. By European standards, gold was common in the Americas, while huge emeralds – a jewel then unknown in Europe – were to be found in profusion. Gold was put to all manner of decorative and ceremonial uses, yet to the Indians it did not have the intrinsic value it held for the Europeans: there was too much of it for that to be so.

The great civilizations fell before small bands of Spaniards – Cortes through luck and trickery conquering the Aztecs, while Pizarro's band of just 168 men achieved an audacious and still scarcely believable victory over the might of the Inca Empire, albeit an Empire conveniently debilitated by civil war. The spoils of victory were immense. Huge treasures were shipped back to Europe. Small wonder that there was no shortage of adventurers ready to come and seek their share of this seemingly inexhaustible hoard in other, still-unexplored parts of the continent.

The search for El Dorado has its origin along the north coast of South America, an area which is now divided between Colombia and Venezuela. Its origins are confused, as its name indicates – because in Spanish El Dorado does not mean "golden city", it means "golden *man*". Indeed, there was such a golden man. He was the ruler of a people called the Chibcha, who lived on a high plateau near the present-day Colombian capital of Bogota. Their holy place was the circular Lake Guatavita – the product of an ancient meteor impact – and every time a new chieftain was appointed he had to undertake a ceremony of appeasement to the powerful god who was thought to live under the lake's surface. He would anoint himself with gum, and then would be covered from head to foot in gold flake, seived from the rivers which carried them down from the gold-rich mountains. The golden chieftain then rowed alone to the centre of the lake, and immersed himself in its icy waters until all the gold was washed from his body. When he returned to shore his people would shower golden objects into the lake, which is still reckoned to have a fortune in gold at its muddy bottom.

Stories of the golden king of the Chibcha filtered through to the Europeans, and during the 1530s various expeditions set off in search of this man, this El Dorado, and the fabulous realm he was assumed to rule. They endured enormous privations, as they struggled their way through hot and hostile country. There was malaria and yellow fever. There were other killing diseases spread by flies and other insects. There were jaguars, vampire bats, and savage tribes, some of them cannibals. Many died. Ambrosius Dalfinger's expedition of 1531-3 was not untypical: a hundred and seventy men set off, but only thirty-five returned.

By 1539 the Chibcha had been discovered, and their treasure taken from them. But their realm was not grand enough to fit the growing legends of El Dorado. They had no great cities or gold mines (though their land was the only source of emeralds in the continent). The golden man was just the chieftain of a humble tribe; the golden city must lie elsewhere.

The picture of El Dorado solidified even as the city itself seemed to recede further beyond the Europeans' grasp. It was situated by a lakeside, in a valley surrounded

by tall mountains. It was a place whose architecture equalled the best of the Aztec capital at Tenochtitlan or the Inca city of Cuzco. There were great pyramids and palaces, cunningly built of close-fitting stone. Elaborate friezes and sculptures adorned the buildings, depicting the savage animal gods of Aztec and Maya mythology. Its streets were walked by priests and princes dressed in fine and elaborate robes and headdresses. And everywhere was the gleam of gold: sheets of beaten gold sheathing the temples; golden statues at every street corner; gold and emeralds worked into every ceremonial vestment; even flecks of gold in the pavements beneath people's feet. Enough gold – more than enough – to satisfy the avarice of every adventurer on the continent and, nearby, inexhaustible gold mines from which yet more treasure could be hewed without great effort.
But where was it? As more of the continent was mapped, so the supposed location of El Dorado varied ever more wildly. It was on the upper shores of the Orinoco. It was in the Amazon basin. It was somewhere amid the rising folds of the Andes. Wherever it was, it was never found, and after a century of feverish searching – which in its latter stages included Sir Walter Raleigh, on his ill-conceived final adventure – interest waned.

Was there ever a golden city? The accounts are certainly confused, yet what is not in doubt is that there were cities which the Europeans never discovered, particularly in Peru. After Pizarro's men killed the Inca god-king Atahualpa, they installed a puppet Inca, Manco Capac. But after a short while their puppet escaped, to organize lengthy resistance from his secret capital Vilcabamba. The Spanish marched in search of Vilcabamba, but they never found it. The Peruvian hinterland is one of the most difficult terrains in the world – a region of fast flowing rivers in deep valleys between mountains eight or ten thousand feet high, with every inch of land cloaked in suffocatingly thick rain forest. The Spanish found it almost impassable.

It was not until 1911 that American explorer Hiram Bingham, in search of Vilcabamba, was directed by local natives to climb steep cliffs up to where a saddle of land, thousands of feet up, joined two high peaks. There he discovered the famous lost Inca city of Machu Picchu, part of it perched over a three thousand foot precipice, completely invisible and seemingly inaccessible from below. Yet this citadel was not Vilcabamba, still less El Dorado. Even deeper into the rain forest the ruins of another Inca city have been discovered, completely overgrown by vegetation. It is larger than Machu Picchu, and it may be lost Vilcabamba: nobody can be sure.

Whatever the identity of that city, though, who is to say what discoveries still remain to be made in the great tracts of rain forest yet to be explored? Aerial surveys show nothing, but the forest takes over in months or even weeks anything left untended, so a lost city would today be completely shrouded in trees and thick undergrowth. Perhaps someday another explorer will, like Bingham, hear stories from isolated natives and make his or her way to a lakeside region where some curiously regular hills hump themselves out of the forest. Perhaps cutting through the undergrowth and rich subsoil that explorer will find, hidden beneath Nature's shroud, the outlines of carved stone. And perhaps, when the dirt of centuries is washed away, some of that stone will catch the sun's rays and shine with the soft lustre of gold...

Europe's Troy is an historical city brought out of the obscurity of legend; South America's El Dorado is still fervently sought; Asia's lost Shangri-la, remains a folk and religious belief; but in Africa there is simply romance, the romance of the Queen of Sheba and King Solomon, of lost tribes of Israelites, of Phoenician gold ... and the Victorian romance that created the myth of a lost white tribe, still worshipping a proud and eternal Mother Goddess, a Priestess of the Flame: Ayesha.

H. Rider Haggard, more than any other writer, can be credited with making the fiction of a lost city in the mountains of East Africa seem real and still believable. His hero, Allan Quatermain, who discovered the priceless treasure-trove of King Solomon, fought and journeyed his way through most of a continent that, in the nineteenth century was still very largely alien to the Europeans. Quatermain meets Ayesha, of course, but Haggard had already described the realm of She Who Must Be Obeyed in two previous books, of which *She* remains a thrilling and compelling journey of the mind.

After an expedition across the savannah of many days, the explorer-hunters in Haggard's classic novel suddenly see, in the distance, an imposing mountain, its lower slopes forming a sheer cliff. This, they are told, is the house of She Who Must Be Obeyed, an unknown, undocumented mountain in the middle of nowhere. But the mountain has a secret – it is hollow. By following an overgrown and dried-up canal system, built thousands of years before, the explorers pass through the mountain to discover the huge, fertile plain that exists *within* it, surrounded by towering, unscaleable walls of granite. The mountain is a ring, in fact, and in the middle of the land enclosed by it is a city of colossal and majestic ruins; great walls, crumbling temples, spires and towers that have been decaying for four thousand years, all of these surrounded by a deep, weed-racked moat. On the walls are pictograms. But in the streets, only silence and the encroaching jungle.

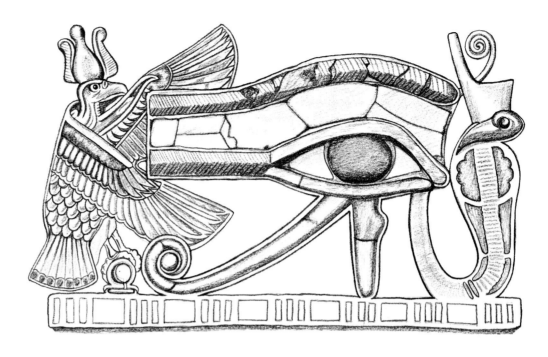

But in the sheer mountain walls that surround the plain is a cave system that dates back to antiquity. Huge galleries and collosal rooms, like cathedrals, are piled high with the mummified dead of centuries, which form great pyramids of bones, most with the parchment skin still drawn across them.

On the walls of these great chambers and palaces that have been hewn from the rock of the mountain are heiroglyphs that seem to antedate Egypt, and pictograms too:

"Love scenes principally, then hunting pictures, pictures of executions, and the torture of criminals by the placing of a pot upon the head, presumably red-hot...There were very few battle-pieces, though many of duels, and men running and wrestling...Between the pictures were columns of stone characters of a nature absolutely new to me; at any rate they were neither Greek nor Egyptian, nor Hebrew, nor Assyrian..."

This strange domain is ruled over by a woman who appears, at first, swathed in veils and silk, hiding her face from the explorers. When she finally unveils she is exquisitely beautiful in an Arabian way, and yet:

"This beauty, with all its awful loveliness and purity, was *evil*. Though the face before me was that of a young woman in perfect health and the first flush of ripened beauty, it had stamped upon it a look of unutterable experience, and of deep acquaintance with grief and passion. Not even the lovely smile that crept around the dimples of her mouth could hide this shadow of sin and sorrow."

Ayesha's secret emerges when she refers to the fact that she has tried – and failed – to teach an ancient wisdom to the Rabbis in the Temple at Jerusalem...years before Jesus came there and was crucified. She is unaware of the final days of the Roman Empire, of Christ's passion and resurrection...she has been isolated from the world around her for two thousand years, and achieves this remarkable immortality by regularly immersing herself in a pillar of fire.

"There is no such thing as Death, though there be a thing called Change. See,' and she pointed to some sculptures on the rocky wall. 'Three times two thousand years have passed since the last of the great race that hewed those pictures fell before the breath of the pestilence which destroyed them, yet they are not dead. Even now they live; perchance their spirits are drawn towards us at this very hour."

A lost kingdom, a chance for immortality – Haggard didn't miss a trick, nor a cliché. It is good, old-fashioned love that destroys Ayesha, so that as she finally steps into the Flame of Renewal her true age shows and she shrivels to a wizened monkey-like corpse.

The idea of exploring an unknown region of the earth and just "happening" across an exquisitely preserved ancient city could have been no less romantic in Victorian days than it is now – and no more likely. As ever, the true wonders of the past are discovered by meticulous excavation and intelligent reconstruction from the fragments and foundations that survive below the creeping earth.

Occasionally, however, the H. Rider Haggard type of dream *did* come true, a real lost city *is* found, in a remarkably intact condition, by careful exploration, and long journey. Of them all, Petra – that "rose-red city, half as old as time" – is possibly the most beautiful, and the most intriguing.

The story of the re-discovery of Petra began in 1812, when a young Swiss explorer called John Burckhardt set out to explore the Middle East. At that time the lands through which he journeyed were violently Moslem – which is to say, violently anti-Christian. Acting with commendable discretion, Burckhardt learned fluent Arabic and conducted his explorations disguised as a Bedouin. Burckhardt did not specifically go to the Middle East to find Petra – his interest was the broader fascination with the kingdoms and cultures that were so effectively hidden from western eyes. But as he journeyed he began to hear stories of a lost city in the hills that had once been in the kingdom of the *Edomites*. The Edomites were a biblical people who warred against the Israelites and disappeared from history about 200 BC. They were superseded by the Nabataeons who built a fabulous city called Petra, carving much of it out of the soft sandstone of a mountain. Petra was a focus for many cultures from the Hellenistic world of two thousand years ago, and the influences of those cultures could be seen in the architecture, in particular of the tombs and temples hewn out of the mountain.

The Romans possessed Petra in their time, and built a theatre, fountains and a spectacular street of columns. But by then Petra was in decline, and after an earthquake had destroyed much of it in the year 350 AD, it was deserted. It remained hidden for fifteen hundred years and the reason is not hard to see. A thousand travellers must have passed by the road to Petra and failed to notice it. When John Burckhardt was at last conducted there he found himself alone – his guides thought of the narrow cleft through the high cliffs of the mountain range as being a haunted place. Burckhardt pressed on, walking through the narrow, dark gorge for nearly two miles. The winding alley through the hills finally opened into a hidden valley, and Petra was there in all its crumbling, yet still visible glory. No lost tribes, no hidden treasures, save the priceless treasure of a beautifully preserved city that had once been the artistic capital of a continent.

El Khazna
Petra

Undersea

Three-quarters of the Earth's surface is covered by water, which means that three-quarters of the planet is for the most part mysterious to us. The proportion of the seabed which has properly been surveyed by humankind is tiny. Any account of the search for ancient shipwrecks and sunken treasure will emphasize how difficult it is to know the world under the ocean surface. Once you go beyond the shallows, sunlight does not penetrate the water. The act of exploration itself stirs up mud and sand from the sea bottom. As you descend the water quickly becomes very cold, and pressure becomes a source of potential danger. It is a dark, murky, chilly, inhospitable realm to a race used to sunlight and heat and air.

Yet to a sea dweller the picture is very different. The seas teem with life, adapting to all temperatures, all degrees of darkness and pressure. Descend into the depths of the ocean's deepest trenches and you will find a bizarre world of grotesque fish life, moving around by the illumination of their own phosphorescent extrusions, the pressure in their bodies equalized to that outside, so that if you bring them to the surface they literally explode. There are the whales and dolphins, possessors

of clearly evolved and complex brains – and possibly the citizens of an undersea civilization, a realm lost to us through an apparently unbridgeable gap in communication. And there are other legends: of cities beneath the ocean, and of humans, or quasi-humans, adapted to maritime life.

The tales of lost undersea cities are often synonymous with the name of Atlantis, to the degree that if any such city were to be found it would almost certainly be named Atlantis by us, whether or not it had any connection with the vanished continent of legend. It does not matter, though, whether the source of such a realm is Atlantis, or some other half-forgotten ancient civilization. All that matters is how such a city might have come into existence, and what it might be like.

There are many tales and legends of civilizations prior to our own – not surprisingly, because human history as we know it covers only a small fraction of the known life-span of *homo sapiens* (which in turn is only a tiny fraction of the known span of life on Earth). Before our most ancient recorded history began, there might have been civilizations which rose, achieved greatness, and then collapsed so completely that only rumours of their existence have filtered down to us across the millennia. There are various reasons for such a fall, among them the geological cataclysms which occasionally in the planet's history alter the shape of continents, creating seas where once there were fertile plains, and thrusting up mountain ranges where formerly lay wide oceans. The geological evidence for such upheavals is all around us.

But it may not have been a completely sudden cataclysm. There may have been time to prepare. And it would be within the abilities of a technologically-advanced human civilization to build cities which would survive the upheaval and enable them to carry on living even after the sea had inundated their land. The obvious solution would be to build domes, since the hemispherical shape would equalize and minimize the pressure on the structure. The domes would be constructed of a transparent material – perhaps some toughened plastic – or might even be force fields, produced by some central generator, though it would require great confidence in technology to pin one's survival hopes on such a system never breaking down for an instant. Inside the domes would be cities, pleasant places full of parks and trees – not so much for aesthetic reasons as for the generation of oxygen; some would be completely given over to agriculture. The citizens of this undersea world would have the sea as their hunting ground, venturing out of the domes in various kinds of submersible, and perhaps in time evolving so that like the deep-sea fish they could withstand the pressures of the deep but could never venture to the surface. Over the centuries the world above the sea – the dry land, the open air, the sun and stars – would become the stuff of myth.

Such undersea cities – be they Atlantean or of some other ancient origin – must be a matter of speculation, though various writers have described alleged discoveries of this kind. The most notable account is that of Captain Nemo, in his pioneering submarine the *Nautilus*, though his Atlantis was a drowned city:

"And in fact, there beneath my eyes, ruined, crumbled and destroyed, lay a town with its roofs caved in, its temples falling down, its arches out of place and its columns lying on the ground. In all these fragments one could see the solid proportions of a kind of Tuscan architecture. Farther on there were the remains of a giant aqueduct; here lay an encrusted mound of some Acropolis, with the floating forms of a Parthenon; there the remains of a dock, as if from some antique port that had once sheltered merchant ships and triremes of war at the shore of an extinct sea; yet further on, long lines of crumbling walls and deserted streets…an entire Pompeii buried beneath the ocean!"

This lost city, whatever its name and origin, lay in a remarkable undersea landscape, possibly the product of ancient volcanic action. Around it were the trees and shrubs of a great forest, now petrified: the stony branches and leaves, lit dimly by light filtering down from the surface, made it an eerie and ghostly place.

Not all versions of the Atlantis myth, however, are as shaped by an image of weed-racked desertion. For hundreds of years – and perhaps even now – the Land Below the Waves was a realm that was fervently believed in. It was part of the plethora of Celtic folklore that included the Land of Youth and the Vale of Avalon: such folklore derives from much earlier times than the Celts, and persists into the modern day with a tenacity that hints at it being more than simple whim.

To the Irish Celts especially, the sea and islands off their western coasts were places of magic and immortality. One of their great heroes, Bran, sailed his small ship west, across the high seas, unaware that Manannan mac Lir was watching him in amusement from his chariot below. To Manannan, Lord of the Waves,

Bran's ship was skimming the clouds. Manannan's chariot races across fields and valleys which to Bran, above, are the glowing realm of Tirfo Thiunn, deep below the waves.

Tirfo Thuinn, like all the Isles of the Blest or Plains of Happiness, was a place of eternal summer and no hardship. Sometimes the submerged lands would be seen to rise above the waves, at which time mortals could set foot upon them. Hy Brasil, for example, rose once every seven years. And Tirfo Thuinn itself was reputed to be suspended by four, huge bronze pillars. Only iron and fire could be used to *keep* such lands upon the sea (iron and fire: the symbols of the Iron Age conquests which – by their banishing of an earlier culture – *created* the folklore that we know so well). Most of these undersea paradises remain to be found – villages off the coast of Wales, Castles a few miles below the waters of Brittany, and golden-turretted cities still flourishing below the Atlantic swell, a few miles from the sheer cliffs of Western Ireland.

In recent years we have seen how undersea volcanic action can quickly create an island of considerable size – initially uninhabitable, but as the surface cools soon seeded with the first plant life inadvertently carried by sea birds. And as land appears, so it may disappear: seismic and tectonic activity may mean that islands from the past have sunk below the ocean surface, carrying with them their people, their buildings, and their secrets. There they may lie, dead or dormant, yet ready at any time to be thrust back to the surface.

This may have been the temporary fate of an area in the remote southern Pacific, a place which in ages past was home to creatures and forces which predated human tenancy of our world. Little is known of those days, yet around the world are instances of groups consecrated to the worship of these "Old Ones". Fragments of information are preserved in various ancient manuscripts, most notably the semi-legendary *Necronomicon*. According to these tales the Old Ones, who may have originated far from this world, were beings who had shape, but were not composed of ordinary matter. Their powers were great, and they could travel both Earth and sky – so long as the stars were "right", a term which suggests some astrological basis for the religion. When the stars were "wrong" they could not live, but neither did they truly die. Instead, they lay in stone houses in their great city of R'lyeh, waiting for the time when the stars again were right, and when someone would come by to release them from their entombment. Of all these Old Ones, the greatest and most powerful was named Cthulhu.

R'lyeh itself was described as a city of strange, cyclopean architecture, seemingly constructed according to some alien principle of geometry; a city now cloaked with aeons' worth of slime and seaweed, lying forgotten somewhere on the ocean floor. Worshippers of Cthulhu around the globe could be heard to chorus a strange chant which, translated, said, "In his house at R'lyeh dead Cthulhu waits dreaming."

These curious fragments of folklore were given unexpected corroboration in 1925 by a sailor, Gustaf Johansen, the Norwegian second mate of a New Zealand schooner, who was found aboard a drifting steamer in the cold southern Pacific. He was the only living man on the ship. He told of how at latitude 47° 9′ S,

longitude 126° 43' W, in the midst of what should have been open and empty ocean, his ship came upon an unexpected island – a shore of mud and ooze with a great stone pillar rising into the sky. Going ashore the crew found buildings of some kind, constructed from huge blocks of greenish stone, and with strangely carved statues and bas-reliefs depicting non-human creatures. His account stressed the peculiarity of the architecture, as if principles unknown to Euclid were in use in the design: as they moved across the stone, verticals would become horizontals, and concavities convexities, without any evidence of transition. The place was impossible for the human eye to assimilate.

After this, Johansen's account became fragmentary and seemingly hysterical. It told of a slab of stone sliding to one side, revealing an abyss within which was an unnatural darkness – not so much an absence of light as its negation. And from that darkness, he claimed, came a creature which destroyed the rest of his crew: a giant creature not dissimilar to the image found on carvings used by worshippers of Cthulhu...

There is one final aspect to the tales of undersea realms and peoples, and a very curious one, namely that in most respects they reflect very accurately sober predictions of the directions future undersea exploration and colonization might take. How can this be? Could it be that in some way which we do yet understand, these are distorted racial memories not of our past but of our *future*? The rational response is to dismiss this as absurd: how can we remember, in any way at all, that which has not yet happened? It goes against common sense, and the evidence of

our senses. Yet one thing which we have learned from twentieth century scientific developments – particularly in quantum physics – is that the evidence of our senses is of little help in defining and understanding the nature of the universe.

The future which we can predict, barring catastrophe, is one in which the sea plays an increasingly important role, most particularly as a source of food and minerals, but also as a habitat. How better to work at farming and mining the oceans than by building cities in their midst? Such cities might float on the surface, like gigantic oilrigs, but as we know even the most stable oilrig can meet disaster in freak weather conditions. It is much safer to go down to the ocean bottom, where there is no weather to contend with, and where there is safety and stability, as long as one avoids seismically unstable areas! Such a city on the ocean floor might be composed of a series of domes, which maintained inside a pleasant and quite spacious habitat. In the vicinity fish and suitable undersea plants would be intensively farmed, the fish kept in place by ultrasonic "fences". Once the technology was developed such habitats would not be inordinately expensive to build or maintain, and would quickly become self-sufficient. In the event of some catastrophe, such as nuclear holocaust, destroying life on the surface, the undersea cities would live on, and in due course life on dry land might be forgotten... It is easy to see in this scenario echoes of the tales of forgotten underwater cities; and indeed the wheel would come full circle, because if a city of this kind were built what could it sensibly be called, except Atlantis?

Mermaids

A common and persistent myth or traveller's tale concerning the undersea realm is that of human or semi-human creatures adapted to maritime existence. Mythologies of course often describe gods of the sea – deities such as Neptune/Poseidon, who rule over the underwater kingdom. Other such stories cannot be accounted for as elements of a religion. Tales come from all parts of the world, and date back hundreds or even thousands of years, and they are very consistent in their detail. They refer to the creatures we have come to know as mermaids.

Mermaids are human from the waist up, and are generally beautiful, with long hair which they like to comb as they sit on rocks by the water's edge. Below the waist, however, they are fish-like, scaly, with powerful tail-flukes like those of a whale. There are also tales of mer*men*, naturally enough, but they appear to be both uglier and wilder, and are rarely seen by ordinary humankind.

There are reports of mermaids growing to immense size – up to 160 feet in some early Celtic descriptions, one such creature having been washed ashore and measured over a thousand years ago; its fingers were each seven feet long. But for the most part reports talk of beings of normal size.

Accounts also differ concerning the friendliness or hostility of mermaids – which may simply mean the mermaids differ in their attitudes to land humans. Some reports speak of mermaids luring seamen to their deaths by singing siren songs to guide them on to rocks, in some instances going further, killing and even devouring the sailors. In other accounts they are friendly, but elusive, accompanying ships but keeping their distance.

According to Scottish and Irish tales of the roane and the selkie, there are beings who can change their shape: when they swim in the sea they are like seals, fast and sleek; on land they are like ethereal, beautiful humans. The offspring of a

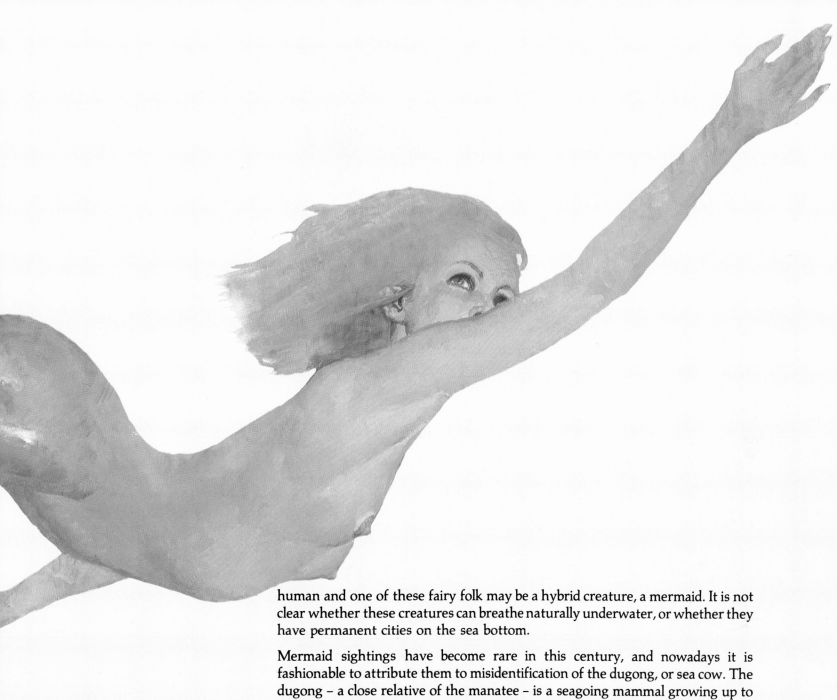

human and one of these fairy folk may be a hybrid creature, a mermaid. It is not clear whether these creatures can breathe naturally underwater, or whether they have permanent cities on the sea bottom.

Mermaid sightings have become rare in this century, and nowadays it is fashionable to attribute them to misidentification of the dugong, or sea cow. The dugong – a close relative of the manatee – is a seagoing mammal growing up to eleven or twelve feet in length, which has a habit of basking while floating on its back (and also suckling its young in that position). Such a creature, it is argued, might easily be mistaken for a quasi-human female by sailors starved of female company through spending months at sea. In theory this sounds plausible, but the problem is that if one actually *looks* at a dugong – which for all its amiable nature is an ugly and not at all humanlike creature – it is difficult to imagine even the most desperate sailor seeing it as a beautiful woman. Moreover, the dugong is a native of the Indian Ocean, whereas mermaid sightings are very widely spread through all the seas, except in very cold latitudes. It is more plausible to believe that mermaids are, or were, a quite different species – one which today has either died out, poisoned, perhaps, by the pollution we pour into the oceans, or has gone into hiding from the human race. It would be easy for intelligent sea-going creatures to conceal themselves in the vastness of the oceans.

Underworld

From the earliest of times there has been a fascination with the idea of a dark world below the earth, hidden from human eye. That such realms existed was probably never in doubt. Caves extended deeply into mountains. . . they had to go somewhere. Gorges and crevasses appeared in earth and ice, leading down into the cold, silent world below. And rivers bubbled up from subterranean depths, leading away from the shadow realms beneath the hills. Very early in time this Underworld became associated with a more religious "dark", with evil and with punishment. In the earliest stories told of these lands below the earth lies the genesis of later myths, and it is that growing body of myth which becomes the powerful religious imagery of the Middle Ages. Across the wide earth, cultures contrast a Bright Heaven – a place of idyll, freedom and reward – with a Dark Hell, a shadowland of pain and cold and emptiness.

The motifs that characterize the Underworld vary greatly, but certain almost archetypal images are associated with the subterranean realm from cultures as remote from each other as the Americas and the Aboriginal peoples of Australia. There is the concept of the "buried" ocean. There is the all-pervading darkness. There is the idea of a vast river that somehow separates the realm of the living from that of the dead. There is the belief in a primitive life continuing out of sight of civilized man. These archetypes pervade the imagination, perhaps drawing from a collectively unconscious memory accrued in the remote days of the first humans.

But what *was* that memory? Does it recall a time when access to the world below the earth's surface was easier? Or when visitors from that realm – loosely referred to as Troglodytes – were more common? Or does memory survive of an actual *place*, a buried or hidden kingdom, briefly visited by early Man, a place that gave a single genesis to the whole genre of Underworld myth and fiction?

What feeds the legend? What continues to engage the fancy? For fascination with the Underworld does not diminish and even twentieth century fictions – undaunted by the knowledge of Earth's molten interior – continue to romance about lost subterranean worlds. Does legend, and do more modern fictions, contain clues to the nature of an archetypal under-realm that might still exist? In this chapter we survey several of the more dramatic works, both from the past and the present. We offer clues but no conclusions, hints but no certainties. The readers must judge the evidence for themselves.

Despite titles to the contrary, few novels are concerned literally with the *centre* of the Earth, dealing rather with the possibility of concealed kingdoms and landscapes in the solid continental masses which float upon the liquid magma. Jules Verne's *Journey to the Centre of the Earth* is a superb documentation of a journey to such a realm. Professor Lidenbrock takes his party into the earth by way of the extinct volcano Sneffells Yokul in Iceland. Following the cryptic directions left by a mediaeval explorer, Arne Saknussemm, the expedition descends through the crystalline galleries that honeycomb the earth's crust. They emerge at length onto the shores of a huge ocean, stretching away below a cavern of immense size, whose phosphorescent ceiling illuminates the waters. They are a hundred miles below the earth's surface in a world where prehistoric marine animals contest viciously for dominance, where huge mushrooms and ferns form petrified forests, where the bones and tools of prehistoric man litter the shores of islands within that great sea.

"A vast sheet of water, the beginning of a lake or an ocean, stretched away out of sight. The deeply indented shore offered the waves a beach of fine golden sand, strewn with these little shells which were inhabited by the first living creatures... From this gently sloping beach, about two hundred yards from the waves, a line of huge cliffs curved upwards to incredible heights... It was a real sea, with the capricious contour of earthly shores, but utterly deserted and horribly wild in appearance."

Verne's novel is that of a scientist, with human involvement well subjugated to a series of scientific lectures. Verne does, in fact, explain in great detail how such a subterranean world could exist, explaining origin, oxygenation, light and the survival of life. But central to the novel are the *location* of his world – below Iceland, the North Sea and Scotland – and the image of the ocean.

More often than not, fiction relating to the Underworld locates the entrance to that realm in the cold, arctic wastes, and the lands themselves below those desolate reaches of the northern hemisphere. Charles Derennes, for example, describes the so-called North Pole Kingdom in his *The People of the Pole*. The sub-polar inhabitants are civilized dinosaurs, derived from one of the smaller lines of early reptiles. They exist in a maze of ice tunnels, occasionally emerging onto the arctic wastes.

The land of Pluto, however, lies even deeper. "Pluto", of course, is the mythological name of the dark Lord of the Underworld (applied, also, to the darkest, coldest planet in our Solar System). The name, interestingly enough, also means "riches". The subterranean world of Pluto is reached through chasms in the Iron Mountains surrounding both North and South Poles, and exists in the hollow crust, warmed and illuminated by light from our own Sun, which filters through cracks in the earth's surface. Pluto is described, in an anonymous source published in 1821, as a land much like earth, but where everything is much smaller. Here, then, may be the original source of such creatures as the Leprechaun.

Plutonia, described in Vladimir Obrutcev's 1924 novel of the same name, is reached through a deep chasm in Fridtjof Nansen Land, north of the great

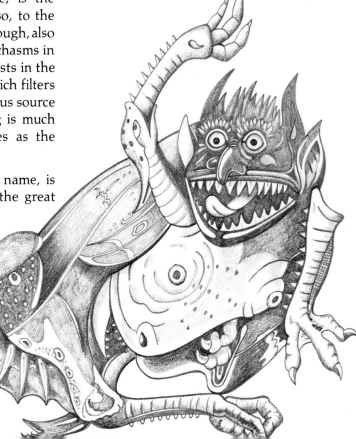

Russian mountain chain. Plutonia and Pluto derive from the same archetypal myth image and may be the same world, for Obrutcev describes the primitive life forms that are to be found there, mostly mammoths, prehistoric animals of various sorts, and dinosaurs. From the Black Rock desert rises an immense extinct volcano, whose forested slopes support an intelligent ant-like life-form of gigantic size. This image of a "World Mountain" is potent, powerful and primal, and features repeatedly in Underworld myth and story, as well as in legends of the lost place of the Ancient Wisdom (see LOST CITIES).

The subterranean realm of Pellucidar is another world deriving from the myth image of Pluto. Edgar Rice Burroughs describes Pellucidar as existing 500 miles beneath the world's surface, and lit by its own sun, which brilliantly illuminates the rising curve of the land, creating the dizzying sensation of standing on the inside of a vast bowl. A satellite round the sun casts a permanent shadow on a part of Pellucidar called The Land of the Awful Shadow. Entrance to Pellucidar is through a concealed passageway at the North Pole. The subterranean realm has several vast oceans, on whose islands live a bewildering variety of primitive forms of Humankind, mostly still at a Stone Age level of development. Their names are colourful: the cannibals of Azar; the madmen of the Valley of the Jukans; the warrior women of Oog. To most Pellucidarians all other races are mere myths.

The catalogue of subterranean world goes on: Protocosmos, a gigantic island floating below the surface of the earth on molten liquid and looking *up* to the glowing earth's centre, which it imagines to be its sun; Atvatabar, which lies below America, stretching from Canada to Ecuador; Aglarond, also known as the Glittering Caves, which are extensive grottoes below the mountain of Helm's Deep, described in great detail in J. R. R. Tolkien's *The Two Towers*; and so on.

And England itself is not without its subterranean counterparts, whose basic image – including a strong theme of mindless obedience – seems to draw from an unconscious memory of a much older realm.

The so-called Roman State lies beneath Northern England, its nature and its inhabitants are fully described in Joseph O'Neill's *Land Under England*, as does the buried land of Vril-Ya, located more specifically, underneath Newcastle, which is featured in Lord Lytton's *The Coming Race* of 1871, and is altogether a more pleasant version of the subterranean kingdom. As with many versions of the legend, Vril-Ya is reached through a deep mine, which opens into a gas-lit roadway. The roadway continues downwards for many miles and ends in a building of Egyptian design through whose decorated pillars a wide, bright valley can be seen. Unlike the slave population of the Roman State who have been brainwashed into a state of mindless servitude, the people of Vril-Ya are tall and beautiful, provided for by the Provisioner of Light and possessed of a sophisticated technology based on an energy form known as Vril. So popular was Lytton's book, that when a new health drink was launched, it was named after this energy form: Bovril. The land is richly forested and teems with life, including reptiles of enormous size, tigers, and birds of strange species whose singing is quite exquisite. Like the robotic inhabitants of that barren realm that lies below Hadrian's Wall, however, the Vril-ya exist in a state of tranquil equilibrium because of the denial of their right to question the past or the state of things.

And it is in this way, this sense of a ghostly existence, that they echo one of the residing images of the Underworld as expressed in the various mythological stories that have been condensed into our modern, rather cynical view of Hell.

We cannot know what sense of an Underworld existed in Paleolithic times, but we can be fairly sure of one thing: there was a fear that the dead would come back to haunt the living. Thus, the dead were buried in the ground – the realm of the worm – and tightly bound to prevent them moving until they had rotted away. The fact of this trussing-up of the dead can be established from the way the bodies lie, knees drawn tight to the chin, arms crossed. So at a very early stage, the Otherworld was associated with *below earth* and with *imprisonment*.

In increasingly sophisticated symbols, this idea of imprisonment can be seen in the more advanced civilizations that followed. In the Assyro-Babylonian myths – of Gilgamesh and other Man-Gods – dating from the third millennium BC, there is the "infernal dwelling place", known as The Land of No Return. It lies beyond the abyss of Apsu, below the earth. This dark kingdom is guarded by seven walls, with seven gates and fourteen demons. After passing all seven of these barriers a voyager finds himself in the dwelling place of shadows and there is no return. In this infernal land exist the captive gods, good and evil genii – or guardian spirits – and of course many adventuring heroes, for the myths were as much the stories of the day as they were a part of the religion.

We find the same notion of inescapability in both Egyptian and Greek Underworld myth. In the Egyptian concept, the "infernal land" is wound around by an immense serpent – an almost Universal symbol, echoed thousands of years later in the Norse Middle Earth myth, the Midgard Serpent. In the Greek version the way to the Underworld is across the nine loops of the River Styx, making this lost realm hard to enter... and hard to leave. Imprisonment, a concept of levels of difficulty involved in the reaching of the place, consecutive barriers against the hidden realm, and once there the Universal fixation with a subterranean sea, feeding rivers that reach to the surface of the world.

Again, in the Finno-Ugric stories of the "infernal region" we find that to reach Tuonela – the land of Tuoni, or the Underworld – a journey of many weeks is required, passing through thickets, then through woods, then forests, then across a river with black, billowing waves. Tuonela, in these ancient myths of the peoples of Russia, Lapland and Finland, is not a place of punishment, but from it the spirits of the dead cannot escape, although it also appears to be a storehouse realm of magical lore. The hero-figure, Vainamoinen, successfully enters and leaves the Otherworld after seeking the magic words for the building of a great ship on the surface ocean. In Tuonela, too, we find another potent image: the guardian beast, in this case the monster known as Surma, which guards the abode of the goddess of graves. Surma has its kin in the great multi-headed dog Cerberus, which guards the gates to the Greek Hades, in the monstrous dog Garm, which guards the way to the Norse Underworld of Niflheim, and in the demons and giants that guard the way to Scathach's realm, or Annwyn, the dark sides of the Celtic Otherworld.

The duality of the Underworld, the idea that it has both a light aspect and a dark aspect, is another primal image that seems to be a clue as to where and what the

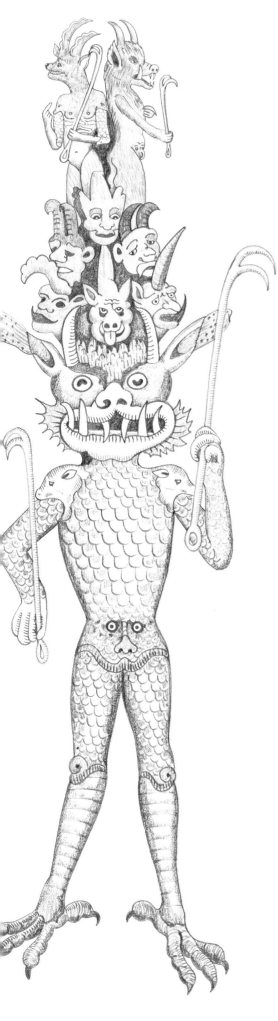

original lost realm of the Underworld might have been. In Egyptian mythology the notion is very simple. The Sun God, Ra, sails his boat from East to West across the heavens by day and at night enters the endless caverns of the Underworld bringing brief light to the inhabitants of that dark abyss. Tuonela is described as a land darker than the surface land of the living, but nevertheless the sun *does* shine, albeit darkly, upon the silent, shadowy inhabitants. In the Greek concept of the world below the earth we also have a "double" realm, and we have a similar concept of the insubstantial nature of the dead as in Tuonela. The Greeks saw the souls of the dead as pale reflections of a once-glorious living body, insubstantial, tenuous shades, devoid of courage and energy, the very essence of lifeless. In Greek myth, too, the concept of the Underworld is linked with the idea of a great lost *city*, known, in this instance, as Tartarus. Tartarus was the Underworld realm to which were condemned those who had committed a crime against the Gods. A sombre, eternal gaol, entered by a bronze gateway and surrounded by three great walls and the waters of a great river, within Tartarus is punishment of awful nature, such as is seen with Sisyphus, eternally condemned to roll a rock up a steep cliff. But contrasted with Tartarus are the Elysian Fields, where the souls of the "just" can enjoy a perfect climate, and an endless idyll such as is normally reserved for the Gods.

Duality exists, too, in the Celtic Otherworld, the contrast between Avalon, the Bright Realm with its endless feasting, fighting and rebirth, and Annwn, where live the silent dead, unable to communicate with the heroic visitor from the mortal world. Annwn is a shadowy realm, though parts of it border on the Celtic dream of unlimited wine, food and fights. The Irish equivalent may be found in the Kingdom of Scathach, which is protected by demons and horrors of exaggerated unpleasantness, all of which must be subdued before the Otherworld may be entered... or left. In the Celtic world view, where honour and the warrior-ethic were all important, it is not surprising to find the Underworld visited by rampaging hero-figures. The modern equivalent would be a tale of an elite SAS group storming the gates of Heaven. A similar lack of awe is found in the Norse epic-myth cycles, and it is also in the Scandinavian concept of the realm of the dead that an interesting dichotomy in the conventional view is found.

The world, to the Teutonic peoples, including the Norsemen, was a place of three realms: the Abyss, from which the earth and the realm of Man was formed, a place given the name Midgard or Middle Earth; Niflheim, to the north of the Abyss, an eerie world of clouds and shadows; and to the south of Midgard, the realm of Muspellsheim, a place of fire. Waters of ice from Niflheim combined, in the Abyss of Midgard, with poison waters from Muspellsheim and created solid layers of hoar-frost. The hoar-frost melted and from the drops formed a giant, named Ymir. Ymir died and the surface of his enormous body became stone, and formed the Earth as we know it. In the rotten flesh formed maggots, which the Gods made into the dwarves. These were relegated to the subterranean spaces. Mankind was formed from two lifeless trees which the gods Odin, Hoenir and Lodur discovered on the corpse of the stone giant. The trees were given warmth, colour and reason; one was called Ash, the other Vine, and these were the first man and woman.

Yggdrasil

The Teutonic peoples have a third concept of the world, its heavens and subterranean hells, however, and it is perhaps the most memorable. It is the idea of Yggdrasil, the World Tree. Yggdrasil is an immense Ash tree, with its branches reaching to heaven, its trunk forming the world as we know it, and its three roots reaching down to the three worlds below.

One of the roots stretches down to the realm of the Aesir, the name given to the Gods Odin, Vili and Ve and their offspring. It was the Aesir who had killed the giant Ymir: they had formed Middle Earth from his corpse by using his blood for the lakes, his flesh for the soil, his bones for the mountains, his teeth for the rocks and pebbles. In this realm, below Yggdrasil's first root, lay the Well of Urdr, whose waters were concerned with "Fate". Three Norns guarded the Well, using its waters to refresh the Ash Tree itself.

The second gigantic root of the World Tree reached into the Land of the Frost Giants. Beneath this root was a spring whose waters gave wisdom to all who drank it. There was usually a penalty, however, and though Odin managed to drink at the spring, he lost an eye as payment.

The third root passed downwards to the realm of Niflheim, the kingdom of the goddess Hel, which was the land of the dead. The spring that was the source of all rivers gushed from Niflheim – again, an association of the Underworld with

rivers, and very comparable with the Greek vision of the rivers Styx, Lethe and Acheron all flowing through Pluto's Underworld, and all associated with different "effects" like the springs below Yggdrasil; to drink from Lethe, for example, was to forget the past.

Yggdrasil was considered to be fighting a constant battle against its enemies, the spirits, serpents, stags and demons that, in their various ways, all were trying to destroy it. Goats, for example, nibbled at its branches and young shoots – even Odin's great horse browsed the foliage. But more insidious than these, below its roots lay a huge snake called Nidhoggr, which constantly gnawed at the tender wood. In the branches of the tree perched an eagle, and this and the serpent were deadly enemies. They used a squirrel as a go-between to send insulting messages to each other.

What a lovely symbol of nature at war with itself the Ash Tree is. It represents a memory of the earliest times of Humankind, when the forests and the beasts of the forest had to be subdued, and many things in nature were seen to be magic. And Yggdrasil too symbolizes regeneration; after ragna-rok, the Doom of the Gods, all the Gods save Baldr will be killed by fire, and all men and women too, save for Lif and Lifdrasir, who will hide in the trunk of the Ash and emerge from the Underworld to repopulate the earth.

Faerie

The popular modern idea of the Realm of Faerie – or Fairyland – has been shaped to a large extent by Victorian and Edwardian depictions. This is something of a tragedy, because that picture is often distorted and trivialized; the true Realm of Faerie is stranger and wilder, more varied and more dramatic than anything the Victorians imagined. It is a world coexistent with our own, yet separate from it; a world invisible to our senses, except on the rare occasions when a human is given access to Fairyland. But while the world of Faerie is beyond our perceptions, the reverse is not true. Its inhabitants know the pathways which link the two worlds, and can pass through them at will.

But who or what precisely are the fairies? In the widest sense the name can be used to describe every sort of supernatural or magical being lying outside the compass of religion – everything, that is, except angels and demons. But this includes all manner of monsters and creatures from folktale and legend. More specifically, they are beings "of a middle nature between man and angels" – as they have been described – generally human in form but varied in their size and habits. There are tiny fairies, and fairies of human – or more than human – size; there are fairies who live on land, or under water, or beneath the earth; there are fairies who are civilized and those who are wild and alien. They call themselves by many names, such as "the Good Folk" or "the Strangers".

Their origin is uncertain. Some claim that they are spirits of the dead; others that they are the remnant of some race more ancient than humanity, a race which perhaps once dwelt openly in this realm, before our spreading domination led them to retreat into their own land. Alternatively, they may be thought of as spirits or beings who are less than gods, but more than ordinary humans. Perhaps they once were gods, but their power has dwindled, so that they now dwell in a land halfway between the human world and the world of the spirits.

Pathways into the faerie realm are to be found everywhere and nowhere. A traditional way for a human to gain access is through a fairy ring – an area of grass curiously marked around its perimeter. If one enters and dances, one may leave the ring to find a different world outside. Entrances may be found between bushes, or in woodland – rarely or never in buildings – but the person who is not aware of them or is not looking in the right way may pass by a thousand times without seeing anything, let alone crossing the threshold. It can only be crossed by the right person at the right time looking for it in the right way.

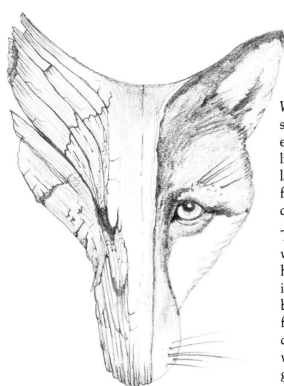

What such a person would see would be no more than a glimmer, a hint of something strange at the very edge of their vision. As they passed through the entrance nothing would at first seem different, though the flowers might seem a little more colourful, or the woodland a trifle lusher. But as they moved along the landscape would become different: a wilder realm, a place where the ancient forests had not been cut down, where the land had never been tamed by cultivation.

The pathway is like a funnel, with its narrow end poking into our world – which is why it is easier for the fairies to pass into the human realm than *vice versa*: they have access to the wide end of the funnel. Sometimes, too, it functions as though it channels space itself, so that as a fairy creature passes from its world into ours it becomes smaller as the funnel narrows – this is one explanation of why some fairies are so tiny in our world. Looking at such a pathway from the other direction, it seems that the further one ventures into the funnel, the larger is the world that is revealed – although its action is such that humans do not become giants in Fairyland.

A typical account of a visit to Fairyland through such a gateway is the tale of Elidor, which was recorded by Giraldus Cambrensis in the twelfth century. Elidor was a twelve-year-old boy who liked to play truant, hiding in a hollow in a riverbank. Once, when he had been absent for two days, two small men came to his hiding place and invited him to follow them to their country. The path, at first dark and underground, led to a beautiful land – a place of rivers and meadows and woods. There were no moon and stars, though, so the nights were pitch dark, while the days were cloudy and dimly-lit. The people were noble and kind. Elidor went to and fro as he pleased, for a while, but as is so often the case in these stories greed brought about the end of his idyll. His mother – in whom he had confided – persuaded him to bring from Fairyland some of the gold which was common there, so Elidor stole a golden ball belonging to the king's son. But when he returned home he dropped the ball, and the two fairies whom he had first met saw what he had done, and were angry, and took the ball away. When a contrite Elidor tried to find the pathway again he could not, even though he searched for a year. For him the entrance to Fairyland had been permanently closed.

The people of Faerie in this tale are representative, in that they are friendly towards normal humans, until their trust is in some way betrayed. Then they do not forgive, but withdraw forever from contact. Such benign fairies – sometimes known as the "Seelie Court" – may indulge in some harmless trickery, but they

are not cruel. In *A Midsummer Night's Dream* we see such fairies playing tricks on each other as well as on an innocent mortal. No harm is done. There *are* malign fairies – called the "Unseelie Court" – but thankfully they appear to be in a minority.

It is rare for a human to visit the faerie realm except at the behest of its inhabitants. The pathway must be shown to us if we are to find it. Sometimes human children are taken captive, to be raised in Fairyland and often to become fairies themselves. In these cases a changeling may be left behind to confuse the human parents – either an inanimate object bearing an enchantment which makes it appear human, or a sickly fairy child, or an elderly fairy. It appears that the faery people are not very fertile, so that they must sometimes supplement their population from human stock. There are also tales that the evil fairies may take children for a more sinister purpose, that of sacrifice, but again these are uncommon.

Children or others taken into the Realm of Faerie may be affected by one of its strangest aspects – the fact that time there does not flow at the same rate as it does in our world. Nor is there a simple relationship between the two – one cannot say that a month in Fairyland is a year in our world, or *vice versa*. It seems to work both ways. There are tales of people falling under fairy enchantment and travelling to their world, and dwelling there for long periods, only to return home and discover that but moments had passed. Often they will not have aged in the faerie realm, so that it is as if they had dreamt the whole thing (and as we know, dreams can seem as though they last a long time when in fact they take place in seconds). But there will be some evidence – an object, not of human origin, brought back with them – to prove that the visit was not mere fancy.

More often it works the other way around. A visitor to Fairyland will stay there only for a short period, but will find on their return that many years have passed in our world. They have long since been given up for dead. Their spouses may have grown old and died; their children have grown up. People will not even believe that they are who they claim to be – they are, after all, far too young. Sometimes it may be even worse, particularly if the visitor to Fairyland has lived on fairy food. In such cases the unfortunate person will often crumble to dust when they return to our world and eat their first normal meal. Obviously the substances from which the Realm of Faerie is built are somehow different from the elements which compose our world, and sometimes the incompatibility between the two can be disastrous.

edgewood

In the modern world there are only a few people who have regular contact with the realm of Faerie. Prominent among these are the Drinkwater family, descendants of the marriage between John Drinkwater and Violet Bramble. Drinkwater was an architect; Violet was the daughter of Theodore Bramble, whom Drinkwater heard speak at a Theosophical Society gathering, where he explained the relationship between the two realms as he saw it:

"'The world inhabited by these beings is not the world we inhabit. It is another world entirely, and it is enclosed within this one; it is in a sense a universal retreating mirror image of this one, with a peculiar geography I can only describe as *infundibular.*' He paused for effect. 'I mean by this that the other world is composed as a series of concentric rings, which as one penetrates deeper into the other world, grow larger. The further in you go, the bigger it gets. Each perimeter of this series of concentricities encloses a larger world within, until, at the centre point, it is infinite. Or at least very very large.'"

Drinkwater soon enough discovered that Bramble's knowledge of such matters was more than just theoretical, and after he married Violet he became known as more and more of an eccentric, losing much of his earlier reputation in the process. Photographs show them in the company of what appear to be fairy beings.

Drinkwater returned with his wife to his native America, where they took up residence in Edgewood, the amazing house which he designed. John Drinkwater was the author of a standard book, *Architecture of Country Houses*, and Edgewood was built as a kind of compendium of all the different styles illustrated therein. As well as being a bizarre folly it was a sample. People could come and visit and, just by walking around the house, see every kind of style they might be interested in.

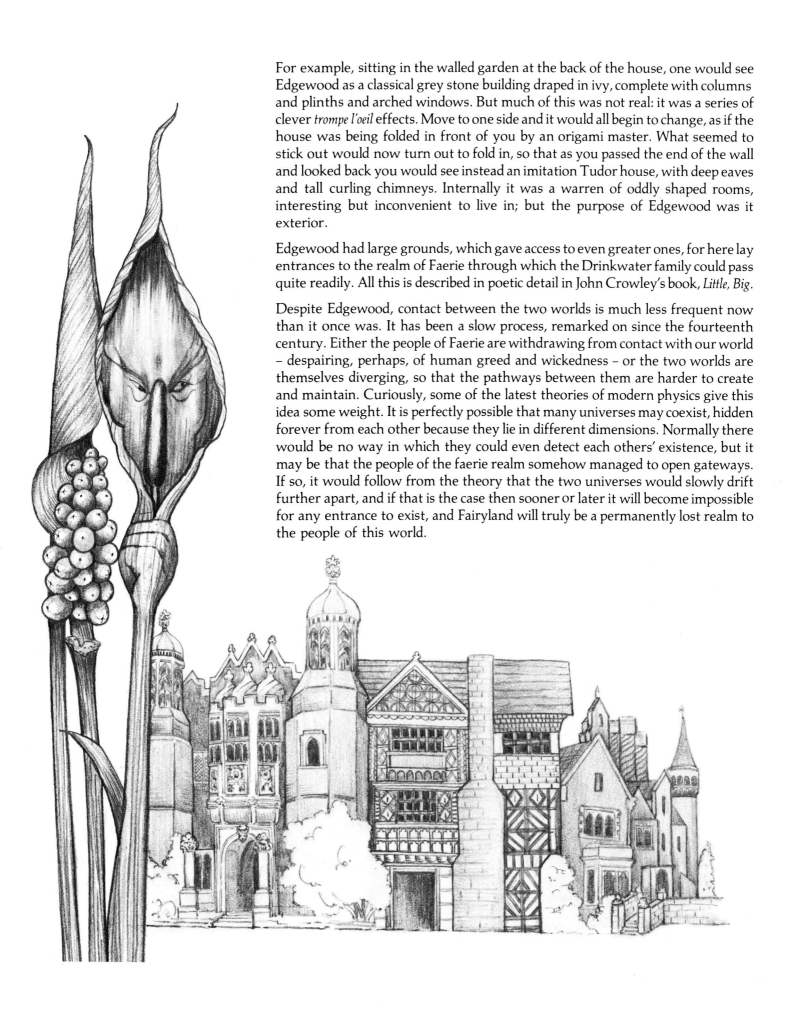

For example, sitting in the walled garden at the back of the house, one would see Edgewood as a classical grey stone building draped in ivy, complete with columns and plinths and arched windows. But much of this was not real: it was a series of clever *trompe l'oeil* effects. Move to one side and it would all begin to change, as if the house was being folded in front of you by an origami master. What seemed to stick out would now turn out to fold in, so that as you passed the end of the wall and looked back you would see instead an imitation Tudor house, with deep eaves and tall curling chimneys. Internally it was a warren of oddly shaped rooms, interesting but inconvenient to live in; but the purpose of Edgewood was it exterior.

Edgewood had large grounds, which gave access to even greater ones, for here lay entrances to the realm of Faerie through which the Drinkwater family could pass quite readily. All this is described in poetic detail in John Crowley's book, *Little, Big*.

Despite Edgewood, contact between the two worlds is much less frequent now than it once was. It has been a slow process, remarked on since the fourteenth century. Either the people of Faerie are withdrawing from contact with our world – despairing, perhaps, of human greed and wickedness – or the two worlds are themselves diverging, so that the pathways between them are harder to create and maintain. Curiously, some of the latest theories of modern physics give this idea some weight. It is perfectly possible that many universes may coexist, hidden forever from each other because they lie in different dimensions. Normally there would be no way in which they could even detect each others' existence, but it may be that the people of the faerie realm somehow managed to open gateways. If so, it would follow from the theory that the two universes would slowly drift further apart, and if that is the case then sooner or later it will become impossible for any entrance to exist, and Fairyland will truly be a permanently lost realm to the people of this world.

land of youth

Before the mediaeval Realm of Fairie became the Victorian "Fairyland", with its flower-pixies and mischievous winged sprites, it was a woodland world where manifestations of nature ruled and held court in the form of Kings, Queens and Warriors. Before that a particularly Elizabethan concept of the Realm it was an invisible land, below the earth or across the wide sea, where magic held sway, gods could be seen, and immortality found for the noblest of warriors. It was, in fact, the Otherworld, the place of the Afterlife. Of the profuse and varied images, and stories, of the Otherworld that survive in the oral tradition into Iron Age times, from 600 BC to about 400 AD, surviving for perhaps thousands of years from what is loosely called the New Stone Age, about 6000 BC, it is the tales of the Land in the West that are the richest and most poignant.

Western Europe populated the oceans towards the setting sun with any number of islands, castles and submarine cities. There was the Land Under the Waves (see UNDERSEA), a beautiful submerged city that was little different from the Beautiful Realm, which itself was a version of the Delightful Plain, sometimes known as the Field of Happiness, The Many Coloured Land and The Land of Promise. More unusual, but richly detailed in the accounts, was Emhain, The Land of Women, an island where there was no winter or want or grieving, and where the golden horses of the sea god Mannannen were the fastest known, and sport and game went on untiringly.

In all of the Celtic lands, too, there was a tradition of a magic and beautiful realm below, or reached through, the great burial mounds of the Stone Age, the tumuli – which in Ireland are so huge that later settlements were built on their tops! Through these so-called *side* the Many Coloured Lands could be reached. Out of the *side* rode men and women who had visited such lands hundreds of years before. Perhaps these adventurers had been pursuing the treasures reputed to be hidden below the mounds, in particular the gold Cauldron of Plenty, whose magic powers are self-evident (the cauldron later became the Grail of the Romano-Celtic cycle). More often than not, however, the returning traveller had been to what is perhaps the most familiar of the pre-Christian Otherworlds: Tir na noc. The Land of the Young.

The Land of the Young lay a long way across the western sea from the craggy cliff coast of Ireland. Sometimes it could be seen, as distant, brilliant glow at dusk, its bright towers and wide fields catching the dying rays of the setting sun. It was to The Land of the Young – tradition tells us – that the Tuatha de Danann, the "people of the Goddess Danu", retreated before the invading Milesians. In this simple legend is a memory of the Bronze Age culture being obliterated by the iron-wielding Celts. The Tuatha de Danann "went into the hills" and from those hills rode their bright horses, raiding and revenging themselves on the people of the new culture. In The Land of the Young they found immortality and peace. Beneath the folk and fairy tales of the Tuatha de Danann, then, is a very real memory of a very early culture. The early settlers of Ireland become the gods and goddesses of the Otherworld.

Overleaf: The myths of the Australian aborigines, which deal with the creation of their universe, are accepted as absolute truth and are the basis of their social and ceremonial life.

In all the stories of these various Otherworldly places there are common themes. The lands are idyllic and beautiful, with the best hunting, the best feasting, the most wonderful music and lovemaking, and glorious battles and duels from which the defeated parties would recover overnight to fight again. In this way, the Otherworld idealises the Celtic vision of mortal perfection.

A second theme, however, is the more intriguing one. It concerns the confusion of *time* in the Many Coloured Lands of the Otherworld. Stories are told wherein, after years on the Bright Plain, hunting great boars and loving many of the beautiful inhabitants of the realm, a satiated and homesick warrior returns to his own world to discover that only seconds have passed since he went away. This inversion of time, however, is the rare one. More commonly a real case of relativistic time distortion is hinted at as the returning traveller discovers that many *hundreds* of years have passed while he has enjoyed but a single summer in the Land of the Young. This strange phenomenon is so powerful a concept that it survives all the subsequent decorations by different cultures, as our contemporary Fairyland is created, and remains one of the great dangers of fairyland in all the more serious stories of the Victorian cycle.

The classic story from the Celtic cycle is that of Oisin – or Ossian – who was one of the sons of Finn mac Cumhaill. One day while hunting he came upon a princess with a perfect body, but the head of a pig. He learned that the woman was truly beautiful beneath the pigs head, but her father – the King of the Land of the Young – had blighted her in this way with but one aim in mind: that she should never marry a warrior, and therefore no son-in-law of the King's could ever challenge him for the throne. Naturally, Oisin accepts the princess's word, loves her, thus returning her to true beauty, goes with her to the Land of the Young, becomes King and lives idyllically for three years. But Oisin grows homesick and returns to his own Ireland through a *side* to find that three hundred years have passed and he is a legend. He has been told that as long as no part of him touches the ground he will be safe, but from horseback, reaching for a horn to summon his brothers from the dead, he touches the ground and becomes immediately old and blind.

A final, fanciful possibility remains, deriving from the knowledge that at very high velocities time, for the traveller, passes more slowly than in the real world. In the images of Tir na noc, of its bright, gleaming towers; of its association with existing below the waves, but rising above them, brilliant by night; of the beautiful, serene people of the realm, who often appear to the Celts and invite them to visit the Otherworld. . .in all of these is an image of a visitation of more alien nature. Were the Celt-ridden lands of England, Ireland and France observed by curious eyes from the vantage point of the wide, obscuring ocean? And did the occasional contact between observer and observed lead to an accidental estrangement in time, a single event of bizarre and frightening consequence that has become embodied in the tales and legends of what we now call the Realm of Faerie?

InterWorlds News Network, Galdate 47698. Wednesday.

HOMEPLANET EARTH LOCATED

Helium-traders discover lost planet by accident

After nearly twenty thousand years as the most celebrated "lost planet" in the Galaxy, homeworld Earth has been rediscovered. First transmissions say that the planet is in the depths of an Ice Age and shows evidence of ancient war. No life of human form remains upon the world. Earth has been a place of myth and mystery for a thousand generations. Although its existence has never been doubted – Humankind began *somewhere* – technoscientific thinking has always held firm that to the belief that the homeworld was destroyed by a solar flare. Despite such gloomy thinking, expeditions by the millions have been mounted in recent times to try to establish the location and nature of the world from whose seas the first life crawled.

The brief through-space transmission from the IFP trade ship *Hail Sophie* was blunt and to the point:

"Nine-planet solar system visited on GD 47697. Strong evidence to suggest third world from sun is fabled Earth. Stellar formation of seven stars visible from system suggestive of animal. First world close to sun, fourth world desert. Third world three quarters water, several land masses heavily forested, polar regions submerged below

MUSEUM OF NINETY WONDERS DISCOVERED ON EARTH

ERU major find during Homeworld Exploration

Everybody knows the story of the Ninety Wonders of Earth. Ninety quests for the magic and mysterious objects of the olden days: talismans, cathedrals, magic bridges, and all of them brought to the Shrine of Sand. We've thrilled to the tales, the adventures against great beasts, robot tribes, earthquakes, and the re-animated dead.

Now, during the course of the exploration of the newly discovered Earth, those ninety wonders have been found. Yes! They actually exist. And far from being objects of mysterious power, they seem to be no more than the museum collection of a group of eccentric warlords, who remained on the planet after the mass migration to the stars..

Protected by a transparent domed covering, out on the desert of the old USA, the collection forms an eerie jumble of artefacts of enormous size. There is the bridge that spans an invisible river. The Ship of Queens lurches heavily beside it. A mechanical clock four hundred feet high still keeps time. Temples from all over the world sink slowly into yellow sand, and the immense hand of some long buried statue holds flame above the desert's surface.

The Museum of Mankind, since forgotten by the solitary men and women who gathered objects from the crumbling of the world. There is something almost sad in the ordinariness, factual basis for one of the most colourful story-cycles

ice. Artefacts and ruins in abundance. World has single large moon, and deserted cities still in excellent condition."

"It is early days yet to start making positive identification," said the Chairman of the Earth Rediscovery Unit on Dragon's World. But the mood is one of excitement. The *Hail Sophie's* discovery lies in the outer spiral sector, a two year flight from the Hub, but the ERU are immediately despatching a twenty vessel fleet to follow up the discovery. In the meantime the precise location of Homeworld Earth is being kept secret to avoid the almost certain tourist rush might obliterate or make difficult the task excavating and exploring the world.

FUTURE

At some time towards the end of the Second Millennium – possibly beginning at that most memorable of mythological dates, 1969 – the Human Race took its first, tentative journeys into space. Within a generation there were mining colonies on its sister planet, the Moon. By the turn of the century the immense planetary system of which Earth was a part was undergoing an intense phase of study. The first voyagers to the nearer stars followed, and with that event comes a second magic date, ringed around with mystery and romance: 2277 AD. Legend, or historical whimsy, no-one knows. But quite possibly that particular date marks the beginning of Humanity as a Galactic Settler.

And then what happened? The atmosphere of Planet Earth changed catastrophically, the result of its fragile shell being so repeatedly punctured by space-shuttle after space-shuttle, ferrying people to the starships. Then the barren earth itself cracked open. Deforested, demineralised, agriculturally devastated, the very planet itself began to reject Humankind.

By the Third Millennium Earth was a deserted place, a lifeless world. Only one in a million of its human inhabitants had survived the eco-disaster that laid the planet waste. Although the fabled Seven Clans remained, the rest of the survivors went out to the new and prosperous worlds of the Far Stars.

The Seven Clans that remained scoured the ravaged planet, gathering all that remained that was beautiful, or useful, or memorable. This became the legend of the Quest for the Ninety Wonders, but it was originally probably no more than a simple exercise in scavenging. . .

Stated bluntly like this, the end of Earth seems unexciting, almost depressing. And yet these simple facts are the only historical facts that can be gleaned from the whole immense body of myth, legend, fabrication and idle folklore about Old Earth that abounds in the Galactic Network.

Those stories are rich, wild and wonderful. Many of them seem to allude to earlier legendary tales, with ancient heroes being dressed up in more modern guise. The Quest for the Ship of God stories are a prime example. Although varying considerably from world to world, the essential story, of a young Space Pilot discovering an alien memory bank and programming his ship to take him into the Under Realm of Space, remains the same. His search for the Sacred Spaceship which had brought God to the planet Earth in the earliest days of the Human Race simply reflects an age old search for some holy icon. The gathering of his twelve Night Riders, the search for the legendary Starcastle, on the lost world of Lyona, the war against the Byorx in which the space pilot Arven triumphs, and his final betrayal by Mederen his clone-brother, seems to draw upon a much earlier myth cycle, possibly relating to the fabled Kennedy family.

Overleaf: *Exclusive first transmitted chromo of Earth Museum of Ninety Wonders.*

But where is Earth? Where is the homeworld that Arven so desperately quests for in the stories of The Seeking of the Twenty Gods? Arven dies on the fringes of a strange star system, crying out "I can see the blue remembered hills", and sends his ship with its alien memory back to the aliens who made it. His Night Riders discover all manner of lonely outposts of Humanity and magic in the sun systems they explore, but all turn out to be worlds *pretending* to be the Mother World.

Only two facts seems to emerge from the folk tales of Arven, two simple pointers to the location and nature of the homeworld solar system. One is the reference to the quest for the system of "twenty gods". Earth was part of a twenty-planet system, whose names still ring with mystery: Mars, Jove, Satan, Titan, Venaza, Phobe, Callistera, Io, Deimosa and all the rest. The other pointer is the continual allusion to the "seven limbed bear" in the heavens. This is always taken to refer to the constellation of seven stars that had been shaped like the extinct animal, a bear. Arven seeks in the Library of Star Views for such a stellar conformation but finally finds it carved on the black marble of dead Thracia. "Thracia" is the old name for Cygnus 39, the world sterilized by a solar flare. There is indeed a continent made out of black marble, but Arven's carving has never been found.

To find a convincing formation of seven stars would be a strong guide to the location of Earth. In the meantime, stellar explorers base their location work on the "twenty gods".

But were there *really* twenty planets in the solar system? Two things begin to throw doubt on that assertion. One of the fundamental guides to Old Earth is crumbling.

The main doubt comes from the study of the recently discovered *Larousse fragment*, a part of a book made out of *paper* (a fibre and clay based material) and printed in pre-Stygian glyphs called an *alphabet*. The *Larousse* is a collection of myth and history believed to be based largely on fact, and the fragment so far translated deals with the history of the continent on Earth called Greek. The people of Greek believed in many gods, sons and daughters of gods, and manifestations of the gods. Among these latter were *titans*, and the names of the titans include *Iapeta* and *Rhea*, the names of two of the twenty gods, or worlds.

But one city above all speaks straight into legend. The original Shining City, standing in the middle of a desert, its massive protective dome gleaming with phosphorescence. Within its cover, a life of sorts continues: robot life. Primitive, repetitive, nevertheless each morning the city wakes, transport runs, houses are cleaned, and all the autonomic functions of the self-contained living place go on without hitch. It is an eerie experience for the Documentation team of ERU to walk the silent streets, and see movement and activity in the absence of intelligent control.

If the people of Old Earth *had* called the other planets of their solar system after these older gods, *is it likely that they would name planets for minor deities?* Jove and Satan were true gods, but Titan, Rhea and Iapeta were not. *Could these have been the moons of a smaller number of worlds?*

The translators of the *Larousse fragment* make their feelings clear. There were not *twenty* planets in Earth's system. There were *four*: Mars, Jove, Satan and Io. Four true planets; and all the rest merely satellites.

But to go from twenty worlds to four may also be too extreme. The inhabitants of the planet Schaafsma's World, orbiting Altuxor, have just been contacted after a time of isolation of fifteen thousand years. Clearly of Earth origin, the Schaafsmana appear to be descended from an original and sole settlement, perhaps just a single colony ship. There *is* influence in their society from more technologically advanced worlds, but macrocyte-antigen and glial-cell surface scan studies suggest that no interbreeding has ever occurred. As such, the folk tales of the Schaafsmana go *directly* back to Earth.

Among their stories is the Legend of the Eight Wonderful Flights of the Fire Eagle.

The Eight Wonderful Flights of the Fire Eagle

There was once an eagle that had the heart of a man and wings of the hardest metal. In its belly it had fire and in its head it held all the memory of the world. The eagle had built its eyrie in the desert, and sometimes it would fly so high above the land that it could settle upon the forests and valleys of the silver island that flew above the hills.

One day, as the eagle was sleeping, it was brought a fragment of a great egg. The egg shell was bright coloured and made of marble. On its outer surface were strange words, and the eagle was intrigued by them. Somewhere in the land was a bird that was greater than the eagle itself. There would either be war or comradeship, and the eagle set off to find the bird who had laid this strange egg.

First the eagle flew to the Island of Fire, where nothing could live because of the great sky furnace that scalded the mountains and valleys of the land below. Then the eagle flew to the island of Clouds, and spent a year flying above its valleys, seeking the bird that had written the strange signs on its broken egg. Then the eagle flew to the Island of Red Wind, and spent a year searching in the shifting sands and below the great ice fields for the other bird.

Overleaf: first transmitted chromo of Shining City on Planet Earth

By now the eagle was tired, but it flew to the huge Island of Cloud Storms, and spent five years searching among the whirlwinds for the other bird before travelling to the Island of the Rainbow. Here it rested for ten years, below the great rainbow that spread above and below the island. The land here was cold and dark, and the islands hostile and surrounded by raging seas. It flew, then, to the Island of the Titans, and then to the Island of Green Ice, and found nothing. At last, weary, cold and dying, it flew to the smallest island of all, so far from its own land that it was always night. This was the Island that led straight down to the Underworld, and the eagle found what it was looking for. The Island was covered by great machines, all frozen and preserved in ice. There were strange buildings, and eerie gateways, huge chasms in the ground, and all across the valleys lay the fragments of egg shell with the strange writing upon them. Here, though, no bird was to be found, but only its tomb, a tall pyramid so high above the land that the eagle could hardly fly to its top; it stretched so deep into the underworld that its roots were in Hell itself.

The eagle was too tired to fly home. It stared from the top of the tomb into the black void of the Underworld. Its search for truth had brought it to death, and it accepted death readily. It flew into the darkness and never returned.

The "eagle" is an extinct bird of Earth, although eagles existed on several worlds until quite recently. But the name "eagle" was given – according to some sources – to the very first space-ship launched from Earth, presumably because of its similarity to the majestic bird! When the Schaafsmana talk of eight wondrous flights, are they alluding to the exploration of the original solar system? The egg with its strange markings which the eagle seeks... could that be a fragment of alien technology? The description as being like a marble egg sounds very like the spherical tomb-urns of the extinct G'chathraga aliens. Were the G'chathraga watching Earth from the most remote of its planetary neighbours?

The eagle flies to eight islands. The first island is bathed in fire... a planet very close to the Sun? One island is bathed in clouds, which sounds like a greenhouse effect. One island is dry and windy, a typical geologically decayed world. The rainbow is a clear reference to a ringed planet. And the island of cloud storms clearly indicates a giant world.

If the eagle legend *does* go back to antiquity, then it is very possible that we should be searching for Earth in solar systems of *nine* worlds, and not twenty or four. And from one of those systems there is an animal-shaped star pattern in the sky. The second planet from the sun is covered by clouds. The sixth planet is ringed. All of which may be nothing but whimsy. But it is surely worth some small investment of time and energy to at least *scan* the Galaxy for such systems. And there may be another clue in the Schaafsmana culture. A warrior culture, the horselords of the clans carry round shields. The pattern on the shields is always the same: a double spiral, a representation of a spiral galaxy. And about a third of the way from the edge, in the outer spiral, there is an eye. "The Eye of the Mother", their protective divinity. Certainly, there is no reason why this simple symbol among the millions of apparently ancient references to the old world and way of life should be afforded more importance, but it is at least a beginning place!

Further Reading

AVALON
King Arthur's Avalon by Geoffrey Ashe
The Glastonbury Legends by R.F. Treherne
Le Morte D'Arthur by Sir Thomas Malory
The Death of King Arthur translated by James Cable
The Mabinogion translated by Jeffrey Gantz
The Celtic Realms by M. Dillon and N. Chadwick
The Bull Chief by Chris Carlsenn

ISLANDS
The Island of Doctor Moreau by H.G. Wells
Gulliver's Travels by Jonathan Swift
King Kong by Edgar Wallace and Meriam C. Cooper

CONTINENTS
Lost Continents by L. Sprague de Camp
Lord of the Rings by J.R.R. Tolkein
The Silmarillion by J.R.R. Tolkein

CITIES
The Ancient Wisdom by Geoffrey Ashe
The Gold of El Dorado by Warwick Bray
Citadels of Mystery by L & G Sprague de Camp
She and *Ayesha* by H. Rider Haggard

UNDERSEA
20,000 Leagues Under the Sea by Jules Verne
The Haunter of the Dark by H.P. Lovecraft

UNDERWORLD
Journey to the Centre of the Earth by Jules Verne
The Coming Race by Lord Lytton
At the Earth's Core, *Pellucidar* and *Savage Pellucidar* by Edgar Rice Burroughs
Gods and Myths of Northern Europe by H.R. Davidson Ellis
The Greek Myths by Robert Graves

FAERIE
Dictionary of Fairies by Katherine Briggs
Faeries by Brian Froud and Alan Lee
Little, Big by John Crowley
Myths and Folk Tales of Ireland by Jeremiah Curtin
Mythago Wood by Robert Holdstock

FUTURE
The Canopy of Time by Brian Aldiss
Nightwings by Robert Silverberg
The Time Machine by H.G. Wells

Acknowledgments

John Avon	*5, 6, 9, 18, 19, 23, 24–25, 32–33, front cover*
Bill Donohoe	*54–72* *painting and border*
Godfrey Dowson	*84–85, 88–89, 90–91*
Dick French	*44, 48–49, 50, 52–53*
Mark Harrison	*16–17, 20–21, 28–29*
Michael Johnson	*72–73, 76–77, 78–79, 80–81*
Pauline Martin	*100–101*
David O'Connor	*34–43*
Colleen Payne	*92, 94, 95, 98, 99, 102, 104–105, 82–83, 86,*
Scitex 350	*Colour illustrations 106–115*
Carolyn Scrace	*96–97*
Grant Bradford	*10–15, 74, 75, 106–115*
	title and chapter lettering, endpapers

Scitex 350, computerised images Steve Hutchings
of The Repro House, London EC1

Karen Hasin-Bromley   *Production Manager*

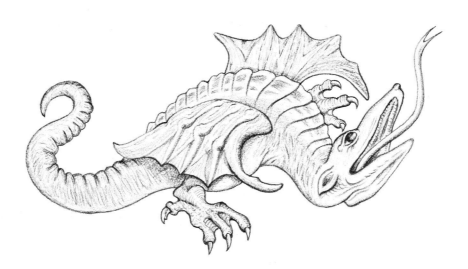

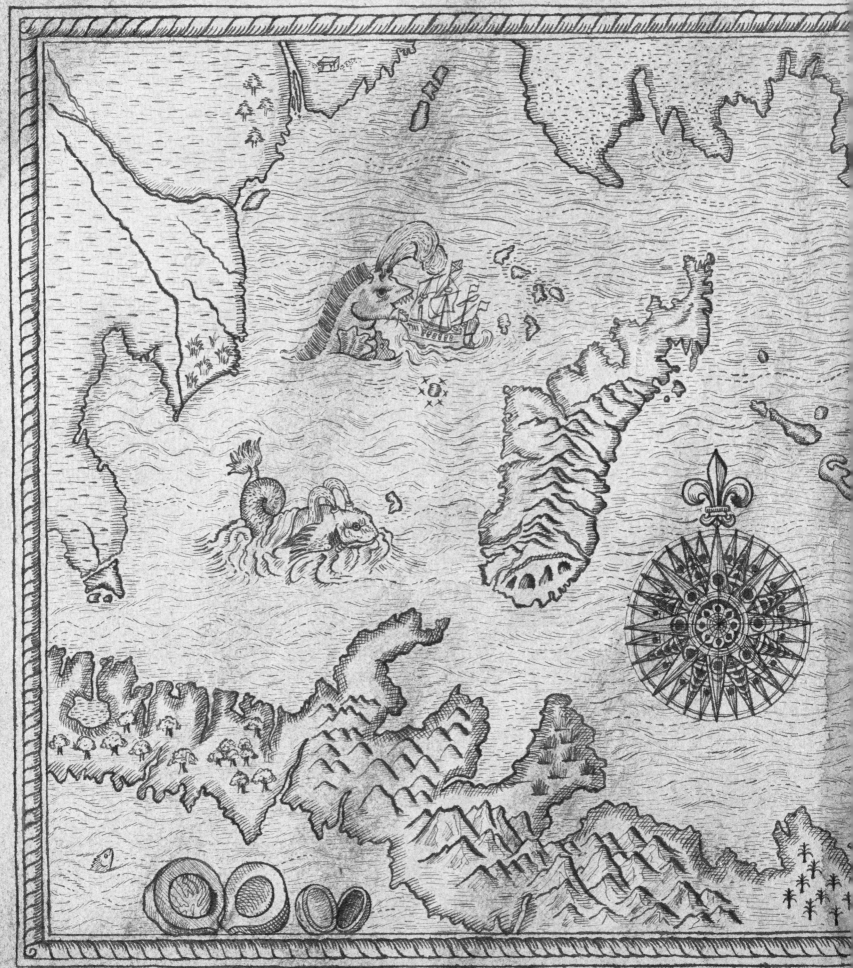

Del. et Gravé par G. Bradford 54.